Comedy

in a

Minor Key

Comedy

in a
Minor Key

HANS KEILSON

Translated from the German by Damion Searls

Farrar, Straus and Giroux

New York

Farrar, Straus and Giroux
18 West 18th Street, New York 10011

Copyright © 1947 by Hans Keilson
Translation copyright © 2010 by Damion Searls
All rights reserved
Distributed in Canada by D&M Publishers, Inc.
Printed in the United States of America
Originally published in 1947 by Querido Verlag N.V., Amsterdam,
as *Komödie in Moll*
Published in the United States by Farrar, Straus and Giroux
First edition, 2010

Library of Congress Cataloging-in-Publication Data
Keilson, Hans, 1909–
   [Komödie in Moll. English]
   Comedy in a minor key / Hans Keilson ; translated from the German by
Damion Searls. — 1st American ed.
      p.   cm.
   ISBN 978-0-374-12675-9 (alk. paper)
   I. Searls, Damion.   II. Title.

PT2621.E24K613 2010
833'.912—dc22

                                                              2010001482

Designed by Jonathan D. Lippincott

www.fsgbooks.com

        1   3   5   7   9   10   8   6   4   2

For Leo and Suus, in Delft

Comedy

in a
Minor Key

I.

"THERE THEY ARE AGAIN," THE DOCTOR SAID SUDDENLY, and he stood up. Unexpectedly, like his words, the noise of the approaching airplane motors slipped into the silence of the death chamber. He tilted his head to one side, squinted his eyes half shut, and listened.

As if a small generator hidden somewhere in the house had started and quickly revved up to full speed, the droning sound of the night squadron flying in grew stronger. It might also—or so it seemed at first—be coming from the basement, or from the house next door . . . But it was the night bombers making themselves heard, no doubt about it. In a wide formation they came from England over the beach that received the North Sea just a few miles away, shot out their flares to show the planes following behind them the flight path over Holland, and disappeared in the night across the eastern border. A few hours later they could be heard in another location, farther north or farther south, returning home, and then their noise grew fainter in the direction of the sea.

The man and woman standing indecisively near the bed, the way people stand when moved by fear and sadness at the same time, also looked up a little and listened.

"Already. So early," the doctor whispered to no one in particular.

Wim looked sideways at him, confused, as though not sure what this comment referred to.

The first shots of the night—dull, thudding pops—were in curious contrast to the fine, almost musical sound of the airplanes. The windowpanes and doors shook and rattled, and the whole house, too lightly built, answered the explosions with a delicate, quick shudder. The beginning was always exciting, no matter how many times a person had already lived through it.

It was near the end of March and the days were getting longer again. When the doctor arrived, around seven o'clock, it was still light out.

Still, Marie had blacked out the windows in the room on the second floor, where "he" lived, as she had been doing for months. This involved a somewhat complicated system of cords and hooks. She preferred to do it herself because she was afraid that someone might see him from the street—a rather exaggerated concern, since there was no house opposite.

Their house stood on the western edge of the city, on

a street of identically shaped new buildings—two rooms with a sliding door between them on the ground floor, three rooms and a bathroom upstairs, and an attic with a crawl space—across from a park. Past the park, the immeasurable west country, with its greenhouses and the pasturelands depopulated by the war, spread out all the way to the horizon, interrupted by canals and dams. Behind that was the mist of the sea. A silver seam out there, like glittering frost, held together the earth and the sky and the water.

This nightly ceremony of blacking out the windows belonged to a regimen of precautions that had moved into their house on the same day as the stranger. When the sickness came too, she performed these actions with even greater care, with a vague feeling that the sick man posed an even greater danger to them than someone healthy.

He had lain in bed for about two weeks. After a year of staying in this room day in and day out had driven the last emaciated traces of life from his face, the fever had given it back a certain color and curvature. In the final days, he spoke hardly a word. It was coming to an end.

When Marie turned on the light in his room in the evening, he still turned his face to the wall, an old habit. In the change from the dim outside light to the flat dull light of the electric bulb, his face appeared gray, like parchment. But his weakened body lay like a lump, motionless under the wool blanket. The lamp at half strength in the middle of the room cast more shadow than light.

Since he had gone into hiding in their house, they had screwed in a lower-watt bulb, to save money. And added a bluish cloth to the milky white lampshade to absorb more light.

Wim and Marie were not fearful people by nature. When they decided to hide someone in their house, they understood the risk they were taking on—to a certain extent, insofar as one can ever judge risk a priori. For risk falls under the category of Surprise, which is precisely what you can't calculate in advance.

What if he suddenly got the idea to open the window himself during the day and stick his head out? Or turn on the light in the middle of the night, after taking down the blackout curtains? Not out of recklessness or to play a trick on them, but . . . You never knew, with a person in his situation, if he was about to do something stupid. No matter how you look at it, it's no bed of roses to force yourself to sit alone in a room, for twelve months or often even longer, always with a certain danger in view, or to shuffle around the room—in felt slippers, of course.

Because for heaven's sake, the cleaning lady who came for half a day twice a week, or the neighbors, could never know that someone was staying here on the second floor. Even if you could completely trust them, "Thank God." Everyone on this street was "good." And who knows if someone else in felt slippers wasn't creeping around in one of these neighbors' rooms too, preferring not to stick his nose outdoors during the day. Anyway, it was better not to talk about such things. There was so much gossip going around . . .

"No one can know, you hear? Only if we agree to that—" Marie had said, back then.

"Of course—" Wim answered calmly. "That's obvious, no one. But you need to think it over carefully, there'll be a lot of . . ."

"I've already thought it over," countered Marie. He should have known that she never did anything without thinking it over. "No one, not even Coba."

"Not even Coba, agreed," Wim confirmed.

Coba was his sister. She lived nearby, in a suburb half an hour away by streetcar. The two women were very good friends, and Coba came by to see them so often that in the long run it was impossible to keep it a secret from her. And really, why keep it from Coba? . . . But Wim had said, "Agreed." They would learn over time. And in the end, every situation conceals within itself certain unforeseen possibilities.

"And Erik?" Marie continued.

"Erik?" Wim asked, taken aback, and again: "Erik?" No question about it, she was nervous. The most nonsensical names were coming into her head. "What makes you think of him? For as long as we've been married, he . . . hold on . . ." He thought about it. "I think he's been here once. There's nothing to worry about with him . . . More likely when Mother comes; what then?"

Marie was startled. "I hadn't thought of that . . ." She rubbed her head with both hands and then fixed her hair again, even though nothing needed fixing. "Yes . . . whenever we have any guests . . . How will Mother take it?"

"So you want to tell her?"

"When she stays with us, Wim—naturally I'll tell her."

"I'm not sure it is so natural," Wim had said, and tugged his tie straight . . .

The first wave of airplanes was now flying over the row of houses.

All three of them stiffened in the same slightly hunched-over position—one never felt totally free. Their heads were tilted a little to one side. As the shots thudded at short intervals now, one after the other, their neck muscles twitched with the tension of listening and with the danger that was hurtling by over their heads, which made the whole house shake in unsteady expectation. The motors pounded powerfully. These artificial constructions of levers and corrugated metal, called to rigid-winged, brief life, filled the land and the sky with the rhythm of their iron pulse.

Here in the room someone had died.

"There they are again . . ." Those had always been his words too. Sometimes, when they would still sit together over dinner in the back room—the only time in the day when he, as arranged, came downstairs—he had suddenly, in the middle of a bite, thrown back his head so that his large, hairy nostrils were visible under the sharply curved ridge of his nose and, with his mouth full, his hands planting the cutlery vertically on the table, he spoke those four words: "There they are again!" It was as if he had been waiting for them.

If the planes came later, when he was alone in his room, sometimes even in bed, he sat up straight and uttered this formula into the silent bedroom.

Of the three of them, he was always the first to hear the airplanes.

Wim didn't let it bother him. "Well . . . ," he answered, more in question than in agreement. But not directly skeptical or denying either. Rather, in the tactful, uninterested way one leaves a matter undecided when it is theoretically possible at some point in time, even if not exactly this one. He certainly never interrupted his meal because of it.

"Yes it's true," Marie said, and hesitated before taking the next bite from the fork she was holding in place —"Yes, Nico's right . . . can you hear it?" She speared her knife into the air.

"So early today," Nico went on, and looked at the clock on the opposite wall. "Ten past seven." His eyes shone because his ears had not betrayed him. The droning grew louder. Wim heard it too.

The first shots of the night—dull, thudding pops—

9

were in curious contrast to the fine, almost musical sound of the airplanes. The windowpanes and doors shook and rattled, and the whole house, too lightly built, answered the explosions with a quick shudder. The beginning was always exciting, no matter how many times a person had already lived through it.

"They want to get back home early; pass the potatoes please, Marie," Wim said. He was satisfied with this dry explanation and felt that he had rid the world of this not particularly interesting situation. "Eat! It's getting cold!"

"No, Wim, no," Nico responded, a little worked up, as though for him it was an existential question, and he let his head with its stuffed cheeks sink forward again until he was looking straight ahead. "No, there are reasons . . . they have a long flight ahead of them, you understand? Maybe Berlin or—yes, it must be Berlin, we are right in the flight path to Berlin here." He spoke with conviction, as though he bore active responsibility for preparing the plans for this night of bombing.

"And how was it for you today, Nico?" Wim usually went on, breaking off then and there all questions of Berlin.

Nico answered in the same good-spirited tone: "Good, Wim, thank you; I am satisfied, the lodgings are good, I practiced my languages for a while, English and French"—or whatever he had done that day.

"How many chess games did you win?"

For he played chess, not especially well but with undiminished zeal.

When Nico had had a good day, he answered this obliquely mischievous question with a similar sort of answer, something like: "None, Wim, not even one. My opponent was too clever for me today . . ."

He always played himself. Hour after hour he sat at the little square table in his bedroom, the board with the pieces in front of him. The chair on the other side of the table was empty . . . e2-e4, e7-e5, g1-f3, and so on. He often sat for a long time with his head in his hand, deep in thought. About a chess problem? Or about ———?

The next day, he could barely wait for Marie to appear upstairs at five in the afternoon with the newspaper.

Hidden behind the curtains he had watched the newspaper delivery woman come quickly across the small front garden. He often left his room just as quickly—in slippers, of course, as they had agreed at the beginning—so that leaning on the banister upstairs, he could hear the newspaper rustle as it was stuffed through the mail slot and then hear it fall onto the stone floor. The seconds that followed next were often the richest in tension and suspense of his whole concealed life. Did they truly understand that, his hosts?

He stood on the last step and waited the short while until Marie appeared from her room, where she would sit, busy with her sewing, at this time of day. She picked

up the paper, unfolded the page, read the headlines—
lies! nothing but lies! but what could you do, you had to
have a newspaper for the groceries—turned it over, read
the personal announcements, the deaths, engagements,
births—even in wartime people still fell in love and
brought children into the world, of course—and then,
still reading, walked up the stairs.

"Nico," she called out, in a half-whisper that even an
eavesdropper would never have been able to hear; only
he could hear it; she knew he was standing and waiting
upstairs —"Nico, you were right again, it says . . ." She
was glad to give him these little pleasures.

But it often happened that she forgot, and Wim was
the first to pick up the paper when he came home from
the office. Or that she was out shopping in the city when
it came.

Then Nico sat on the top step and fought a terrible
battle with himself about whether he shouldn't try it and
carefully, carefully . . . he could take off his slippers too,
creep downstairs in his socks; it would make a small bit
of a difference, surely . . . or down the banister, the way
he used to as a boy—he knew exactly on which steps the
wood gave and creaked, the third and the fifth from the
top, and the first and fourth after the turn in the stairway.

But in the end he didn't dare to do it. Even if he was
convinced that no one, no one in the world, could hear
him . . . It was against their agreement, so he didn't do it.
It was almost too much for his strength. No one knew
what battles raged inside him.

He quickly called to mind something else then, ordeals, the horrors that had certainly awaited him but which he had escaped—to other, new tortures here. "Ordeals and horrors are waiting everywhere," he muttered to himself. "Everywhere."

After a while he stood up and crept back to his bedroom. —

"Well, well," the doctor said as the strikes of the anti-aircraft guns thundered hard nearby, "those are some big ones."

An unending row of night bombers came over the block of houses. It was as though they were flying through every room in the house at once.

He looked back and forth at this wife and husband, felt their suppressed fear of the death that came both quietly and loudly, and looked at the shadow play of the hanging lamp on the yellowish wall of the room.

Then he bent over the bed again and touched the body with his fingers. It was slowly growing cold.

Wim had clasped his hands behind his back, and he stared at the floor. We have to bury him, he thought, of course we do, you have to bury a dead man. But how—?

"A night like this in the bomb shelter, while the house collapses above you . . ." The doctor didn't finish his sentence. Dead is dead, you can die anywhere. And live . . . ?

Marie put her hand tenderly on the curved edge of the high footboard. For her it was like touching the dead man himself. She looked at him. Unshaven and worn out, he lay there with eyes closed. The hair on his head, falling tangled and uncombed onto his bony, low forehead, was black; the whiskers of a beard that had run rampant during his sickness glimmered red. The relaxed, half-open mouth and somewhat hanging chin gave the suffering face a more oval shape. How old he looked! All this together, and her memories of Nico, the man she had kept in hiding in her house, combined into a specific train of thought in Marie's mind. Strange that it had never come to her while he was alive, not like this. She couldn't help thinking of the Bible, even though she was not a church-minded type at all. She thought of the Old Testament, that he was a son of its people. Job could have looked just like that, she thought.

II.

"WHAT WAS HIS REAL NAME?" THE DOCTOR ASKED.

Isolated gunshots still in the distance . . . the same as in the beginning, a humming sound from the house next door, or from the basement . . .

Wim shrugged his shoulders. Even now he didn't reveal the name. It remained a secret. "We called him Nico."

"Nico? Nicodemus? —Wasn't he the only one of the ancient rabbis who . . ."

"Yes, yes," Wim said. "Ours sold perfume."

The doctor made a wry face.

"A perfume salesman? Yes, well, we'll all need a little prettying up after the war. It's not the worst thing. Poor Nico!" His words sounded bitter, almost as if reproaching Nico for deserting them.

Wim pressed his lips together and audibly expelled the air through his nose with a quick jerk of his throat. "Hmmph." A bit embarrassed, they stared at the bed.

Marie was reminded, by the fact that he had been lying there motionless the whole time in the same mute position, that he was dead. A dead man lay in her house, a house in which no new life had yet been born. Over and over again this thought came into her mind. The doctor started to pump the dynamo on his pocket flashlight with his thumb, so that a delicate whirring sound filled the death chamber. The stubby bulb's bright light meandered across the unresponsive face and lifeless hands on the blanket and highlighted individual parts of the dead body more clearly.

"How long was he here with you?"

"Almost a year, he came in April."

"Such a long time? —And how was it? Was he difficult?"

"Not at all," Marie interjected. She followed the men's conversation only insofar as it ran parallel with her own thoughts. "Not at all."

"I see. It isn't always that way. Did you know him from before?"

"No," Wim responded.

"Things happen sometimes, with these accidental combinations . . . We're all only human, and it lasts so long."

"I know," Wim answered calmly. "Not him. It went well. It's such a shame, about Nico."

Silence.

"Yes, well, he can't stay here." The doctor inter-

rupted their silence and stepped decisively back from the
bed into the middle of the room. The husband and wife
followed him.

"Of course not. But how——?" Marie asked, so sound-
lessly that no one could hear her.

"Maybe someone could try to contact the police,"
Wim said. He looked directly at the doctor. He had been
thinking this for a long time.

"The police, Wim?"

"Yes——"

He avoided looking at her. Thoughts whirled in his
head like the airplanes arriving from unknown dis-
tances.

"Wim!"

"The police will get him in any case," the doctor said
airily, and he rubbed his eyelids with his right hand.
"But you have to stay out of it. Then they can make their
arrangements with a clear conscience."

"What arrangements, Doctor?"

"Burying him, of course. ——But now it's still too
bright. I'll come back around ten. It's lucky that it's a
new moon. I'll work everything out with your husband."

Wim nodded. He had understood what the doctor
meant by this talk of the new moon and it still being too
bright outside. Of course, so that's what you did when
this happened. It wasn't too bad. He'd be careful breaking it to Marie. She wouldn't sleep a wink tonight. Still,

what a strange thought, that while you are lying in your warm bed the other man, even if he's dead—or rather, because he's dead . . .

Before the doctor left he went up to Marie, took her right hand in his hands, and said in a solemn voice, "There is no one here to offer condolences to. That's often how it turns out. But still, it must be a loss for you. In fact, you probably have the most difficult burden—problem," he corrected himself.

Marie looked at him calmly. Her face was serious and she thought about what he had said. A problem, yes, but she had happily taken it upon herself. It seemed to her that she had learned something in the process.

"But it's not as dangerous as you think," the doctor continued, because he had the impression that they were still a little frightened. "There are a lot of other things that could have happened. Never mind infectious diseases that we have to report—diphtheria, a child with polio. That is very, very unpleasant. But there are also children born in circumstances like this . . ."

"That's impossible," Marie stammered. It was horrible to think of. Children? Did people have no sense of responsibility?

"Really, it's true," the doctor confirmed, having guessed Marie's thoughts. "I have personally brought quite a few into the world. Four little Jewish babies. Strong boys. They scream just like every child screams when it comes into the world. But that's the danger!

Someone could hear them! The neighbors! In childless marriages, after twelve, fourteen barren years, suddenly there are children born. Naturally they are sent off to other families."

Wim and Marie exchanged a glance and smiled. It might be serious, even slightly sad, but they had to laugh. What couldn't you find in this world! But the doctor was right, children are born everywhere, in bomb shelters, during air raids, and often quicker than you might like. Everywhere, in the grip of death, life goes on too. And in terms of their situation here, it was better to have a dead man in the bed than a woman with a screaming newborn. He was right about that too.

"I have to go now," the doctor said. Wim walked him downstairs.

When he came back upstairs, Marie was standing at the end of the bed by the dead man's feet. He went over to her and together they looked at Nico in silence.

"Wim, do you actually know how Jews bury their dead?"

"What do you mean?"

"Well, they have rules and customs for everything, they must have some for when someone dies." Behind her curiosity there was a burning pain that cried out for more consolation than it was possible to give.

"Of course. I read something about it once." He spoke quietly, whispering, as though it wasn't proper to speak out loud, in front of a dead man, about the way you propose to bury him. Especially since he hadn't expressed any preference himself. Wim considered for a moment, then said, "I think they wash him and put him in a burial cloth with no seams."

"Well, we could wash him too."

"Oh, Marie, let's let it go. Nico didn't follow the laws anymore. He won't hold it against us."

"We don't have a shroud, and I'm sure he didn't have one for himself. Who goes into hiding with a shroud? Or should I look and see?"

"And then they sit with him all night, say their prayers by candlelight—yes, I think they call it sitting shibbe or something like that."

"Hmm. Well, we can't do any of that."

"Beforehand they lay him, when he's died, on the ground, wrapped in a sheet."

"Maybe that, Wim?"

"Yes, Marie, we'll do that."

She took a step back. "Come, I'll help."

"Not now. Let's wait, the doctor is coming back around ten o'clock. He'll help me."

"He's coming again?"

"It's too hard to carry a dead body, you know."

"To carry?" She gestured down with her hand. "Here, on the floor?"

He hesitated. "Not here, Marie."

He raised his hand and gestured in the direction of the window. "We, the doctor and I, will lay him on the ground—in the park. It's a new moon. Under a bench. No one will see us."

"Wim."

A quiet crying rose within her and shook her body with delicate shakes. "No, oh no—yes—what else can we do? . . . Nico, Nico . . ." She held her hand over her eyes. Wim led her out of the room and down the stairs.

III.

THEY USUALLY ATE FIFTEEN MINUTES AFTER WIM CAME home from the office. He had a job as a bookkeeper in a machine factory. In winter, after the time change, he left his office around five o'clock, but either way, summer or winter, they always ate at quarter after six. Both of them, after rather easygoing childhoods, had grown accustomed to doing everything as precisely and punctually as possible. Especially Marie. It gave life, which after all had so many changes and surprises in store, especially in times of war and foreign occupation, a certain fixed form that you could cling to when there was otherwise no shore in sight.

In March, when everything was back to normal again and Marie could breathe easy. Wim left the house at the usual time in the morning, and came home again at the usual time in the evening.

One night in April, Wim said in passing during the meal: "So he's coming today."

"That's good," Marie said, and kept eating. They had made all the necessary preparations for his arrival. But they were both still tense and easily excited.

"A little more soup, Wim?"

"There's more? Sure. But shouldn't we set aside a plate? From now on you'll have to cook bigger portions. There won't be any more leftovers."

"I'll cook big enough portions," Marie said as she handed him the soup, "that we can have hot leftovers the next day at lunch. There will be enough potatoes and porridge as long as there's any at all."

"Do you think he'll eat a lot?"

"You usually get hungrier when you have nothing to do all day but sit and wait from one meal to the next." She waited until he had finished his soup.

"Can we keep eating from the soup plates?" Marie said. She stood up to get the vegetables and potatoes from the kitchen.

"Yes, sure, you'll have less to wash up." She gathered up the spoons.

"Just bring the pot," he called after her.

But she brought, as always, the dinner service with flowers around the edges, which included the deep plates. It was part of her dowry.

"What is he ever going to do with his time?" Wim said. "It's horrible, it's like self-inflicted prison! Maybe he'll study something."

"We go to the lending library too. And then there are

our books. —But who knows if we could stand it," Marie added.

Wim could see that she was already completely used to the thought of it. He still thought back often to their first conversation about it, after Jop—an office colleague who, he assumed, often handled such things—had asked whether Wim ever thought about fulfilling his "patriotic duty" and . . . "Patriotic duty," Jop had said, and the concept, which had never made the slightest impression on Wim before, much less been able to move him toward any action, sounded new and full of meaning, now that the Netherlands had been conquered and occupied. Jop knew the people he approached: with one he talked about "a purely humane act," with another it was about "Christian charity for the persecuted," and to a third he spoke of "patriotic duty." This was how he achieved his goal, the same in each case.

"I'll talk to Marie, Jop. I'm not opposed to taking someone in. We have enough room."

"Almost everyone is doing it," Jop said, to strengthen his resolve. He knew that it was up to the wives. They sat home all day with their guests and had to do most of the work. "A man or a woman, I have to know that too."

"Okay, Jop."

At first Marie hesitated. "Not because I have anything against Jews," she had said. "But to involve yourself so intimately with a stranger's fate, spend all that time under the same roof for who knows how long—

you know that's not how I do things." She was speaking the truth. It corresponded to the shape of her body: medium height, thin, almost youthful, with something cold and dry about it. Only where she loved was there a resonance of deeper feelings, and then she could overcome all sorts of resistance. It was in her nature to make all her objections up front, at the start. This made her a bit slow to take action, but it saved her all sorts of reproaches and resentments after the fact.

Wim was silent. He thought it was a good thing that she was reluctant. They had known each other for around seven years now—he was nineteen when they met and she was twenty-one—and they had been married for three years. She had her own view of things, which was entirely independent and often contradicted his, and she had expressed it in a calm, firm voice. He loved this about her.

"Maybe I'm being selfish, but I don't like this kind of thing. Besides, it's too serious a decision to make lightly."

"Jop says it's a patriotic duty."

She laughed. He had never spoken like that in his life. But when she saw that he meant it seriously, she stopped.

Wim said: "It's the only way we can fight back, the only way we can do anything at all to show that it isn't all right. Civil disobedience."

She thought about the young men who had died in battle, about the five days of the invasion, about Rotterdam and much more. The decision slowly ripened inside her.

"Obviously," she replied, "a refugee like this is not a source of income, at least not for us." She had heard that unbelievably high prices were often offered, and often demanded too.

The next day, after she decided on her preconditions, she agreed. "A man of course. I'll give him the front room upstairs. It's roomy and bright, and if you have to spend the whole day in it . . . What do you think? . . . He doesn't need to stare at the curtain all day. He will definitely have to stay away from the window, I mean . . . Well, we'll see . . . And in the distance there's the ocean, you can see it in the shape of the clouds and in the morning air, it'll be some distraction . . . What do you think?"

It sounded good to Wim.

Jop brought the stranger at night, in the dark, a little before eleven. Marie let them in and Jop quickly said goodbye; he had to be home by eleven, because of the curfew. "Say hello to Wim, I'll come by tomorrow and check in."

The stranger stood in the front hall. He was wearing his hat pulled far down over his face and had a medium-sized satchel in his left hand and a black leather briefcase under his arm. Marie opened the first door on the right, to the front room. All the lights were off. Through the open sliding door, the lights shone in from the back room, where Wim sat busy with some work at the table. Books and notebooks were scattered on the dark brown tablecloth. A teacup sat nearby. The thin, fragrant smoke of a little wood fire fed with peat hung in the room.

When Marie had opened the door for him, he had mechanically, hesitantly walked through the half-dark front room. Marie shut the door behind him. When he saw Wim sitting there, he stopped in the frame of the sliding door, at the threshold to the back room. Only now did he seem to remember that he was inside. He slowly took off his hat.

Wim had stood up and meticulously tightened the cap on his fountain pen, then put it in the upper left pocket of his vest. He saw how the stranger, with an almost unnoticeable motion of his head, had let his gaze stray a little to the right, to the stove. He thought he saw the man's nostrils tighten and then relax again from breathing in the delicate wood- and peat smoke. He wore a winter coat and seemed to be hot from running through the city. There were beads of sweat on his forehead, and his face—dark-complexioned, with little wrinkles around the mouth, and eyes carved deep into his otherwise firm, clean-shaven skin—glittered in the light. His large, dark, somewhat melancholy eyes looked feverish and flickering. His hair was thick and smooth, low over his forehead. A Spanish type! Wim could see that the stranger was older than he was; around forty, he guessed.

"Please come in," Wim said. Nothing else occurred to him besides this everyday phrase. At the same time he invited the man to come closer with a nod of his head.

The stranger stepped silently over the threshold. He carried his suitcase and briefcase as though he were used to keeping them with him. He had his hat in his left hand as well.

Wim took a few steps toward him, stretched out his right hand, and said quietly, as was his habit, "Welcome."

The stranger gripped his hand. They stood close together, both about the same height. "Thank you," the guest said.

Later he let Marie take his coat and hat, so that she could hang them in the front hall, and let Wim set his suitcase and briefcase in a corner. But suddenly he said, in a bright voice, "Perhaps it's better if the coat and hat stay in here for now. I'll bring them along to my room later." Marie turned around in the doorway and looked, embarrassed, at the men.

"That is better," Wim confirmed, and laughed a friendly laugh at her. Turning back to the other man: "You're right. We still have to learn how it's done." Now Marie laughed too. She put the man's things on a chair and fetched some tea.

The conversation was halting. Finally, the stranger, his eyes looking calmer and less feverish, began: "It all happened so fast, Jop had to leave right away."

So he called him "Jop" too. Wim made a mental note.

"He had to get back home on time," the other man went on.

Wim gradually regained his usual composure. Even if he was the younger man here, he was still the host, and that brought with it various responsibilities. He felt that the other man had understood precisely the reasons for Wim's initial discomfort and that he had made an effort to dispel it, even though he found himself in an even less comfortable situation. Wim offered him a cigarette and said, as he lit the match, "My wife and I are happy we can do something for you."

Marie nodded at his words and slowly exhaled the smoke of her cigarette through her nose. She too had fully recovered her poise. Their first encounter had been so confused—the stranger was right, everything happened so fast, Jop had to get home on time. They had needed to make their way slowly back into the trusted port of a safe, well-known conventionality.

The stranger swept his hand over his hair. He could not yet believe he was safe here.

"The conditions in which we find ourselves together here," Wim started up again, "are not exactly of a sociable nature. The purpose of our being together isn't either. We will go through it together, but still, I would like to know your name . . . You must know our names already, yes?"

"In the dark I couldn't read it," the stranger answered, and he seemed a little embarrassed.

They were shocked. "Jop didn't tell you our names?" Wim said. What could that mean?

"No—" he replied, "and it was better that way. Something could have happened on the way here, after all. It's always better if you don't know too much. You have to be careful to the end."

Here he paused for a moment, looked at Marie and Wim, and then said, hesitantly, "So I hope you will permit me to . . . ach, let's use first names, you can call me Nico."

Marie found this surprising, abrupt, even a little rash.

But Wim said, "That makes sense, Nico"—and he extended his hand to him across the table—"That makes sense. In the end we won't be able to stand on ceremony here for long. We have to live together. My name is Wim, and this is Marie."

Marie shook hands with him too.

Then she poured him another cup of tea.

"We also have a place for you to hide, Nico, in your room."

A light shone across his face. All the little wrinkles were lively when he laughed. He timidly began to realize his good fortune.

"We'll show you tomorrow. It's a little complicated—it's too late tonight."

"Good, Wim, that sounds good."

"Tonight there's nothing you need to worry about. No one's looking for you here."

"I'm not scared, Wim."

"If we're a little bit clever, and careful, then you can stay here and there'll be nothing for you to worry about."

"I hope that I'm not causing any difficulties for you—for you and Marie. I don't know how long it's still going to last."

"No one does, Nico. For your sake, I hope it won't be too much longer." Wim stood up. "I think we'll go—"

"Not just for my sake," Nico interjected, and grew serious. Now it was clear that he was much older than Wim . . . "There are so many, so many . . ." It sounded like the simple, honest truth.

Wim hesitated. He understood Nico's tone well. "You're right—for everyone who's in your situation, here or wherever—"

"And it's not just Jews," Nico added. He stood up. He had said what needed to be said!

"That's true too," Wim answered. "Now I'll show you your room."

"Good night, Marie."

"Sleep well, Nico, your first night here . . ."

"What time should I get up in the morning?"

"Yes, when?"—now she hesitated and then smiled a little, with compassion. "Well, you have time. I'll bring your tea up to you."

"Thank you."

Carrying all the things, the two men went upstairs.

IV.

ANOTHER HOUR AND A HALF TO GO!

Wim sat downstairs in the back room as usual. He had shut the sliding doors to the other room. Books and notebooks lay spread out on the table in front of him; he was preparing for an exam, and had been for a long time, so that he could get a higher and better-paid position. At the moment he was taking a break. He had turned his chair a little toward the stove and he had a newspaper on his knee to hold the tobacco for the cigarette he was rolling.

Marie stood in the kitchen and did the washing. She had fetched the underwear, stockings, and other things out of the laundry basket, even though it was so late at night. Whenever it was a question of regaining her inner calm and equilibrium, she did laundry and cleaned the house. Wim knew that. Tomorrow it would be the upstairs room's turn. After all, a dead man had lain there.

Tomorrow, maybe early in the morning, the police would find him too. That is how he would eventually get a proper burial. Later, if someone asked—but who, in God's name! he had no one left!—they could dig him up again and give him a gravestone with his real name. In a moment of familiarity and trust he had revealed it: Bram Cohen, born ———, died ———. For them he had been Nico.

"I want to live to see the end, Wim. What do you think?"

"Why wouldn't you, Nico?" It was long before his illness. "We all want that. And if we don't get a bomb on our roof before then . . ."

In fact, he hadn't meant anything with his reference to bombs. It was a kind of cosmic resignation.

"Do you think they'll still come?" —"They" were the others, on the other side of the Channel. The invasion! He was counting on it!

Wim stuck out his lower lip, raised his eyebrows, pulled his head a little way back into his neck so that his shoulders stuck out more sharply—a face that expressed everything going on inside him: I don't know, Nico . . . (Obviously, who could pretend to know with any certainty) . . . I don't really think so . . . (Better not to count on it, so that you could only be pleasantly surprised) . . . but I hope so . . . (That would finally, finally mean the end of this sh——) . . .

"It's too late now, Wim. —Isn't it too late for a lot of people?"

"Yes, I'm afraid so." Wim had to agree. It was enough to make you lose your patience.

Silence.

Nico sank back into his thoughts. He looked old and gray then, a tired little bird, not at all like a traveling perfume salesman. He got too little fresh air. The few short walks in the evening, in the dark of the new moon . . . He wore old worn-out clothing meant for around the house, just something thrown together, green-gray pants, a blue shirt, mends and patches everywhere on the elbows and knees. He usually didn't put on a tie. By evening his beard had visibly grown back. At first he had shaved twice a day.

"It's lucky my parents were already dead."

"Yes, Nico, that is lucky for them."

"For me too. What would I have done?" After a little while: "They carried off old people, in cattle cars, the elderly, the sick . . . That's not just a story."

Wim knew that too. That is why he was careful not to discuss too fully things that were known only too well. It was dangerous.

"Cigarette, Nico?"

"Thanks."

Light.

"Thank you, Wim."

The first few draws in silence. Then: "This is good tobacco. Where can you still get it?"

And Wim told him the story of the tobacco: "Dutch grown," he said with a grin, "smuggled to Belgium, fermented there and perfumed up with some sort of juice, then smuggled back."

For a little while Nico's thoughts rambled along the Belgian border. He leaned back in his chair while Wim went on telling him about it.

"Whole fortunes cross over the border like that. If the two of us had even half of one of them, Nico . . ."

"What then, Wim, what then?" He would gladly give up his share if that would make the war end tomorrow.

"Last week I talked to a businessman friend from Eindhoven," Wim said, and lit another cigarette. "You wouldn't believe what crosses the border—from illegal people to illegal herds of sheep—everything, everything is transported there and back again."

"In the last war it was exactly the same."

"I wouldn't know that."

"But I can still remember, my father told me about it one time."

"My father," he had said. It sounded so strange coming out of his mouth. It meant at the same time his father's father too, and his father before him, as if someone had accidentally struck a bell and all the other bells began to resonate with it, the bells that over the course of many generations had been cast from the same metal, all the way back to the beginning.

He took a few puffs and contemplatively exhaled into the smoky room. Two, three cigarettes like this in a single evening—what a luxury!

"And if they get caught, Wim?"

"With a herd of sheep they'd lose twenty, thirty thousand guilders. But the next transport makes it up again."

"And for people, when they get caught?"

"It depends whether it's pilots from English planes that were shot down . . ."

"What? That happens too?"

"Of course, Nico. Then they travel disguised as mutes, as a transport of mutes for labor deployment."

They had to laugh when they pictured it: these young, strapping men, a deaf-mute labor deployment!

"And the others?"

"That seems to be well organized too. Anyone who gets across is saved. Belgium is only under military control, there's not a civilian governor like here."

"Are you saying you think I should try it too—?" Nico said suddenly, because he had recently gotten a piece of paper that proved that he was such and such a person. False papers, of course, but still, if you didn't hold it right under the quartz lamp . . . But why, in truth, was he asking? It was his quiet fear. He was always afraid that one day Wim wouldn't answer right away, that he would act like he was thinking it over and then calmly, apparently objectively, say, "That's something you'd have to consider very carefully." He almost expected it. So now and then Nico prodded him with a little test. The feeling came over him like some sort of feverish illness that he was a burden, that the others had had enough of him and wanted to be rid of him at last.

Even though no one had ever given him the least indication of such a thing, these imagined thoughts of the others held him in their grip: "If we didn't have him here, we could . . ." Or: "Well, we have one too . . . it's not so simple. And it's dangerous too . . ." Or . . . It is like a sickness affecting the thoughts of people in hiding, it destroys their naturalness and makes them rude or weak. Few are left unaffected.

But Wim interrupted him: "No, Nico, it's better that you not stick your nose out into the daylight." With all the strict checkpoints! There's a four-hour train ride before you get to the border. Besides, anyone could tell just by looking at him. "I wouldn't take the chance."

Had Nico even heard? Yes, yes, but his thoughts were already racing further. They rode with the trains heading east with no stops, they ran through the camps, those whorehouses of death, slipped into the cells and chambers, saw all the way to the end, to the—

And then he said: "They better be quick about it, Wim, or it'll be too late for us too."

This was the deepest point that he could reach. And he reached it often—only too often.

"Ach, Nico," Wim said, and leaned back in his chair. At the same moment he wished he were sixty and the other man forty. Then it would have been easier. But even so he couldn't have kept it from ending like this—

It was so cold at night. Wim threw wood and peat into the stove, and together they gave off a pleasant warmth that quickly grew stronger. And that delicate, spicy smoke.

Marie appeared in the doorway. She had pushed it open with her elbow and was drying her wet hands on a kitchen towel. Her face shone with effort and her eyes were still red.

"Wim, I was thinking—"

"Yes?"

"I was thinking—maybe you'll think, Why is she mentioning this now?"

"What are you thinking? Just say it . . . Come on, sit down."

"No. I'm not finished in the kitchen yet . . . What'll happen with his things?"

"What kind of things?"

"You know, Nico's—his clothes, his underwear—"

Wim gave out a short, pitying laugh. "Well, he didn't have much."

"No, not much. Should I wash them tomorrow? Or . . ."

"Yes, just wait until tomorrow."

"Coba's coming tomorrow, I'll ask her," Marie said, and she shut the door again. Coba had already helped them often, she would know what to do with the clothes too.

Yes, Coba knew, of course, and so did Marie's mother, and Leen and his friend Leo, who did all sorts of useful things for people in hiding. It could not be avoided—the narrow circle that Marie had imagined at first had been pierced. It happened practically on its own. And so did the other thing. It was unexpected—or maybe not, in the end, totally unexpected. Just a small event, but still a harbinger, an ambassador that the great event, the daily occurrence, had sent as a reminder, since it itself was almost invisible, as if happening between the lines. A wind that also blows in from the sea during the summer, just a little fuller now, and more biting, so that you shiver a little, a cloud that it brings along when September comes, outlined a little more sharply and not so shining and transparent anymore. Or like a faint illness, hardly worth going to bed for, which has already welcomed death into the house.

The three of them had lived together for five months already, wary and often tense, but still, it was normal life. Like every group where one person is dependent on the others, it straightens itself out and finds the guiding star under which everyone can live together.

"He'd rather eat upstairs today," Marie said, still a bit disturbed by what had happened. She poured the thick pea soup into the deep soup plate and put it on the tray, where a glass of water was already standing.

Wim quietly lifted up his own still empty plate, weighed it gently with his fingertips, and then put it carefully down again on the table, a little farther to the left.

Then Marie brought the meal to his room.

"So, you told him," Wim said when she appeared downstairs again. He slowly massaged his thighs with his two hands, and his torso moved back and forth with the same rhythm.

"Yes, this afternoon. He seems to have suspected something like that himself. Suddenly he asked me himself, why—"

"And . . . ?" Wim interrupted her. His impatience betrayed him.

But there was no "And," none at all. Marie put the empty tray on a chair near the door and stepped closer to the table.

They had caught Jop and taken him in three days ago; he had fallen into a trap—he was careless, he was betrayed, who could say? That kind of thing happened, unfortunately, all too often these days. Those were the stakes everyone had to play for if they took part in the game at all. They had searched his house, looking for papers that would incriminate him. Now he was in Amsterdam, sitting in an infamous police prison, and no one knew if he would get through the "cross-examination" alive. He didn't need to say much; people were so modest, they were satisfied with just a little, a tiny little bit of evidence—just the tiniest little pebble, high in the mountains, that worked loose and fell and in falling would grow into an avalanche.

Marie and Wim were warned as well, too late in any case; the danger had already passed. They discussed whether or not to tell Nico the news—whether it wasn't, in fact, better to get him out of their house for a while. Two days later the report came that Jop was in jail with the so-called "light" cases. So there was nothing to fear, for now. But still, you had to be on your guard. That was when they decided to tell Nico.

"Ach," Marie began, "he actually stayed rather calm." She faltered. "He was scared." She fell silent again. It took her a long time to find the words to express what she had, to her horror, perceived.

She had seen fear: the terrible helpless fear that rises up out of sadness and despair and is no longer attached to anything—the helpless fear that is tied only to nothingness. Not fear or anxiety or despair about a person or a situation, nothing, nothing, only the exposure, the vulnerability, being cast loose from all certainties, from all dignity and all love. The man offered it up to her so shamelessly that it felt to Marie like she was seeing him physically naked. No cry out loud, no contortion of his face or his hands, he was simply uncovered, he stood in the middle of the room, the focal point and bull's-eye for all the poisoned arrows being shot at him from beyond life. And Marie understood that words like "love your neighbor" or "national duty" or "civil disobedience" were only a weak reflection of this deepest feeling that Wim and she had felt back then: wanting to shelter a persecuted human being in their house. Like the way people veil a body in fabric and clothing so that the blaze of its nakedness does not blind too deeply the eyes that see it, people veil life itself with precious garments, behind which, as under ashes, the double-tongued fire of creation smolders. Love, beauty, dignity: all that was only put on, so that whoever approached the glowing embers in reverence would not singe his grasping hands and thirsting lips. But wherever violence and annihilation tore away the protective covering, the undaunted heart was thrown into turmoil and could not rest until new costumes had formed, new threads had been spun, to mask and raise up what was shameful and unbearable.

He, too, the man standing so pale before her who had shut his eyes for a moment, felt the look she was giving him. He whispered: "I'd felt so safe here, so safe."

He did not speak Jop's name. But Marie saw that he was still thinking about him and that he had included him in his own—purported—safety and security. She was almost ashamed that she had to be witness to all this.

She had no words for any of it. She said: "He was afraid, of course, for all of us—for Jop, for himself, for us. Maybe not in that order exactly, but what's the difference?"

"Strange," said Wim, "I would have bet that . . . Didn't he say anything else?"

"Should we eat first?"

She sat down. Then she continued: "He suggested to me that he look for another place."

"How could he think such a thing," Wim asked, a

little aggressively. "He wants to just go out onto the street, not knowing where? I hope you told him, Marie."

Marie started to fill the bowls and, in her mind, was already back in the kitchen. She was thinking about the pieces of meat she had always used to put into her soups, which made them so especially tasty. When would they have meat in their soup again?

They started to eat. "I'll talk to him later," Wim said.

"Tonight he won't be coming downstairs again, I'm sure."

"Then I'll go upstairs." Silence. "Did you also tell him that his ration cards are taken care of?"

"I forgot," Marie said, and she let her spoon fall back into the meatless soup. "I never even thought of that."

And Wim said slowly, without looking up, "He won't be eating a single bite of his food up there."

"I'll go right now," Marie cried, a little ashamed, and she flew up the stairs. She didn't stay long.

"You were right, Wim," she announced when she came back to the table, slightly flushed. "Everything was standing exactly as I brought it to him, untouched."

"Maybe it was still too hot for him," Wim said, and he blew on his soup-filled spoon for a long time before carefully bringing it to his mouth.

That evening he had a talk with Nico.

"So what will happen now?" Nico asked timidly.

"Nothing," Wim answered.

He was right. Nothing happened. Jop stayed away

and Leen came by and did exactly the same things that Jop had done. It went on.

More than anyone, Coba proved herself to be a great help. She watched the house whenever Marie had to be away for a shorter or longer time, like the time when Marie's mother fell ill and Marie took care of her for ten days. Coba's nature was just like her walk: not heavy, lightly swinging past every obstacle, but still firm and decisive. She laughed easily. "Excellent!" she said when Marie—during Coba's very first visit—confided in her. "Excellent. How old? That'll work. Older and they're already too fossilized. I had wanted to ask you two for a long time if you'd take someone in."

"Really? Would you have done it too?"

"One? I'd take two or four! Just not three together, that's bad in arguments and so on. It's always two against one. By the way, you don't have anyone else waiting in the wings, do you? I need to take in another three soon."

"You?"

"Yes, well, these things just come up . . ."

Coba—who would have thought it. Marie felt dizzy.

"Does he have visitors? . . . No one? But he needs to see someone else's face now and then." It turned out she had quite a lot of experience in all sorts of useful things. "Careful," she said, "be careful, my friends! But within reason, don't overdo it. That leads to a complex, to anxiety, and that's how mistakes get made. Don't isolate him,

45

fresh air every now and then, when it's possible. Imagine if we . . . !"

Coba and Nico were on a first-name basis right away. She was in her late twenties. The next time, she brought him new books in English and French, detective novels and others.

"When this is all over, Nico, Marie and I get a life-time supply of perfume from you, agreed?"

"Nuit de Paris. Romance for the lady in the evening . . ."

"Not just in the evening, Nico, I'm a lady all day long—"

He went on: "Violetta, Sans-Gêne for afternoons, and some mornings, for fashion shows . . ."

"I've never been to a fashion show myself," Marie said.

The names that used to waft from his lips, sleek and melodious like magic formulas, now sounded perfectly ordinary, and strangely fresh, unused. They too once were, and maybe one day would be again . . .

"Just a drop behind the ear, Marie. Perfume is the visiting card of the lady!"

They laughed. And Nico laughed along with them!

"And what is the white queen's favorite?" Coba asked, with a glance at the chess pieces in battle formation.

"It depends whether she is about to win or lose."

"But Nico? I thought your perfume would help a lady win."

"Well, then you'd have to be playing, Coba, not me," Nico sighed. He knocked over the white queen along with her foot soldiers. Crash!

"I know a pianist"—she kept on chatting, undisturbed—"who's stuck at a table like you. But he's playing a piano."

"At a table?"

"He drew a keyboard on the tabletop so that he wouldn't get totally out of practice. Beethoven was deaf too, after all."

"How long has he been stuck there so far?" Marie asked timidly.

"We're trying to find him a third table now—oak, if we can. He's already played through two others."

"So you're better off with your chess then," Marie said with a friendly nod to him.

"Yes," he agreed, a bit passively, "it's true, I have it better . . ."

Such visits helped, or visits like the ones from Leo, the photographer, who also brought along hair clippers. He came regularly, every three weeks.

"I only do one kind of cut," he said, eagerly rubbing his hands together. "I hope you like it. And if the esteemed client wishes to continue to make use of my services after the war . . ."

He was a teacher of natural science and geography at the lyceum. Nico sat like a patient sheep on the chair and let everything take its course. These visits made him happy. He was cheerful and joined in with everything.

Then he couldn't anymore. Even with clippers, after all, sometimes a clump of hair or dust got in and brought the smooth workings of the blades to a halt. "So here I sit, happy because my hair is getting cut," he thought to himself, "happy, while . . ."

The others noticed. But Leo kept cutting.

Wim and Marie sat in the room during the haircut. They themselves barely escaped the clutches of the hard-working clippers.

At the end, Leo gave an extra show and cut his own hair. But only the right side.

"He hasn't learned the left side yet," Nico teased, and he looked at his own haircut in the mirror for the third time. After the procedure he always felt a bit sad, and lonelier.

"The left side is for the next customer!" Leo said, brushing off his shirt.

V.

THERE WERE PROBLEMS TOO. OBVIOUSLY, WHENEVER
people live together there are problems, like little bombs
with long fuses planted in the gray hours and mostly ex-
ploding at moments when you think everything is going
perfectly. Boom! There's a bang, you're surprised, startled, and a little annoyed; the problems are a burden because they come as a surprise and because you have to
make an extra effort. People who say that they can see a
problem "coming" are like people who say they have a
sixth sense.

One problem was the cleaning lady. She came every
Tuesday and Friday, the same as she had for the past two
years, to clean and scrub the rooms downstairs and
the rooms upstairs, alternating, and the kitchen and the
stairs, and to darn stockings and mend clothes when she
had any time left over. She knew every nook and cranny
of the house and was used to moving freely through it,
working without any special instructions from Marie.

And now, all of a sudden, the upstairs rooms, especially Nico's, were supposed to be "taboo" for her . . .

"To fire her suddenly," Marie said to Wim one evening when they were alone, "would really stand out. I'll cut back slowly."

"I'll just stay in my room," Nico decided. That's what he always did anyway, except for the days when he was so thoroughly bored that just for a change of scene he went faithfully, every hour and a half, like clockwork, to the bathroom on the upstairs floor. "This afternoon too will pass."

"Stay in your room as much as you can," Wim had said at the beginning. "During the day someone or another still comes by to visit. Marie will call you when the coast is clear."

When the doorbell rang, he held his breath for a second upstairs and strained to listen. The milkman? No, he didn't come until around noon. A woman's voice! It must be—he heard laughter and bright voices—it must be—and suddenly the cry of a child's voice between the others, so it must be little Jaap with his mother. Good people, Marie had said, during a friendly hour with him when she had let him in on something about her circle of acquaintances. Good people, but a little simple. Be careful, very careful. Luckily they never stayed long.

Later, hidden behind his curtain, he saw little bow-legged Jaap across the front garden, his mother following behind him while still turned around to talk to

Marie, who stayed in the door to the house. The garden gate was open. Look at that! A horse-drawn wagon! But little Jaapje stayed standing on the threshold and waited.

"Mama, Mama!" he yelled. "Tum!" And he could talk too! He'd really come a long way in the last six months.

"He's calling me to come, I have to go," said Mama, proudly. "Bye, Marie!"

When they were gone, Marie called him downstairs. "Would you like to dry the dishes with me for a change?"

"I'd like that, Marie."

He stood downstairs in the kitchen, carefully took the plates and cups in his left hand, and wiped them all around with his right, which held a cloth all crumpled up.

"You don't need to press so hard, Nico. Like this . . . softer . . ."

The next time it went better. Marie could wash so fast that Nico fell behind with the drying. Plates, cups, and pots piled up on the green rubber mat.

"Slower, slower, Marie, I can't keep up."

Marie laughed. She just did it automatically; it was as if the plates and bowls flew from the boiling sink water onto the table. "Wim is totally at his wit's end when he helps me," she said. "He says he gets dizzy just watching." She held the big aluminum pot for boiling potatoes in the water, turned it all around so that little sprays of water fell on the stone counter and into the basin, while working on the inside of the pot with a wire mesh scrubber. "You can't buy what you need to clean pots with anymore. It takes twice as long. You can feel the war even in the kitchen, whether the pot is full or empty. Always the same old story."

She poured the dishwater out and grabbed a cloth to wipe off the basin and clean out the drain. Then she helped him dry the rest of the dishes. "And then I'll make us a cup of coffee."

A sojourn downstairs like this was like a trip to another country.

One time he went downstairs himself, without thinking about it, when he smelled burned milk in his room and throughout the house. Marie must have gone out to get something; she must have been planning to come right back and had put the milk on the stove in the meantime. The smell was getting stronger every second.

When he walked into the kitchen he ran into Marie at the stove. Nico was startled. "Oh, I thought . . ."

"What's wrong, Nico?" It sounded a little surprised, but still perfectly friendly.

"The milk smelled so strong."

Then the doorbell rang and Marie went to answer the door. Nico stayed behind in the kitchen. The burned milk had boiled away into a dark brown crust on the black stovetop.

The fishmonger stood outside with a big woven basket full of his fresh catch on the stoop in front of him. A rare opportunity! She always let him into the kitchen, where he cleaned the fish. Marie couldn't send him away, he would never come back again. And they all liked to eat fish. But now Nico was in the kitchen.

Marie was confused and left the fishmonger standing there, ran back into the kitchen, disappeared behind the closed door, and said in a whisper, a little indignant, "The fisherman, Nico—but where can you go? Shhh, keep quiet. Your voice—" Nico stood pressed against the kitchen table and looked at Marie, full of distress. What should he do? Go out to the back garden? He couldn't do that either. God, that stupid milk! Did the fisherman really have to come right then?

Finally she had a saving inspiration. Right next to the kitchen was a toilet, with a door opening onto the hall just to the right of the kitchen door. The hall itself was a good fifteen feet long and the fishmonger stood at the other end, with the big woven basket under his arm, getting ready to leave. Marie decisively opened the bathroom door and directed Nico with a hand gesture out of the kitchen and into the bathroom, whose wide-open door blocked almost the whole width of the hall, covering Nico's escape. The half-moon on the door turned to "Occupied." "Come on in!" Marie called to the fishmonger. Let him think whatever he wanted.

It took half an hour for him to scale and clean all the fish, get his money, and, after a little chat, disappear from the house. Nico stayed locked in the bathroom the whole time.

"You could have quietly gone upstairs," Wim said that evening when they were sitting at the table together and discussing the incident. Nico felt that he was on some kind of trial, even though both the others took the event in good spirits and didn't give it any overexaggerated significance.

"But then he would have known for sure that someone was there."

"He knew that anyway."

"But someone who lives upstairs, Wim . . ."

"Why not?"

"?"

"Why shouldn't we have a lodger?"

"Hmm."

"You know, Nico, we all have to make an effort to act as natural and unaffected as we can."

Nico looked down at the table, and his fingers drummed a muffled melody on the tablecloth. Finally he said, in a clipped voice and with pauses between the words, "Of course, Wim—you're right—it was only because of that stupid milk—"

"Nico thought I had left—and he wanted to save the milk." Up until then she had been careful not to intrude into the conversation between the men. After all, it was uncomfortable enough for Wim already, him being a young man and the other a good deal older. When she said this, she looked directly at Nico and was amazed to notice how agitated he was getting.

"I thought, it's so hard to get milk nowadays, Marie."

"Well yes, it is. But still, it's better . . ."

"Next time I'll just let it be," he blurted out all at once, and he stopped his drumming on the table with a light blow of his fist. "I'll just stay upstairs and let the milk do whatever the milk is going to do."

"And I'll make sure," Marie replied pointedly, looking with great interest at the picture above the stove as though she were seeing it for the first time, "to turn the gas off in time."

No more conversation. Painful silence. Nico already felt bad about his light blow to the table. But he sat as if nailed to his chair and looked pleadingly from one to the other.

"Yes," Wim said with his unshakable calm, and he pulled strongly on his cigarette, "maybe it's best if we keep everything the way it was before. Everything worked out fine, after all. Marie will call you when she thinks you can come downstairs. When you're managing a household there are always surprises."

At least someone had said something. Nico exhaled with relief. This calm, this good-natured calm he had! Marie also felt her annoyance slowly fade away.

"And then," Wim continued, leaning far back in his chair like a father holding forth before his big family, "then I won't think that you were—shall we say—trying to criticize Marie."

"Not at all, Wim," Nico agreed. He positively hissed

out the words so as not to let a second go by in which the others might possibly believe the contrary. "Not at all." He looked over at Marie, his eyes open wide, his face tense and nervous. His hands were shaking too.

She felt sorry for him; in fact she saw his whole state of mind clearly and saw how much more he had to lose than she with her vanity about being a good housewife. But it was only with difficulty that she found the words to lighten his burden.

"It happens sometimes," she whispered, and tried to smile.

Even though it was not clear what exactly she meant—her mishap with the milk or Nico's—it was enough for him to hear that her voice had changed. It was over.

She stood up to serve the tea.

.

"Good," said the cleaning lady. "It's a good time for me too, to go to once a week. No, I won't look for anything else. All that bending over. The likes of us have bladders too. And livers." And hers were not in good shape. She was a working woman, stuck alone at home with six children, four girls between twelve and eighteen years old and two boys, seven and ten.

"So you'll only need to clean our bedroom every three or four weeks. Then you won't have to climb so many stairs."

"Good," the woman answered.

Nico stayed motionless in his room on those days. He heard the woman's footsteps stomping heavily through the house, heard how she carried the laundry into the bedroom, how she moved around with the vacuum cleaner and carried out her other duties. The nearness of another human being, even one who he knew harbored no suspicions, stirred up the tense quiet and solitude of his room.

Then, at around four o'clock, Marie came upstairs with a cup of tea. She had been able to arrange it so that she poured the cup in the kitchen while the woman was taking a break in the living room, sitting tiredly on a chair and drinking her own tea. Marie only had to come to the door and give the signal by knocking, and Nico opened the door a sliver, took the teacup, and immediately shut the door again. On the other days, Marie brought her own cup along and they sat together and chatted. So the weeks went by without the woman noticing that Nico was sitting in his room.

Once, in mid-October, on another Tuesday when the cleaning woman was in the house, Nico heard someone slowly coming up the stairs at around four o'clock. Marie with the tea, he thought, and stood up. Why is she taking such deliberate steps? Maybe she's carrying her tea, or some laundry? . . . He crept to the door and waited. The steps came closer; now they were on the last landing of the staircase . . . right up to his door. There was something tense inside him. It's Marie, I'll take the tray from her. He carefully opened the door.

Before him stood the cleaning woman. She was carrying a laundry bag and breathing heavily. Her gray hair was disheveled from working and it hung down to one side and over her forehead into her yellowish gray, slightly puffy face. Her pains were back, and while she was climbing the stairs with the load of laundry, bending forward to put pressure on the stabbing pains in her body, her thoughts had drifted to the wrong door. She held the laundry bag pressed tight against her chest and looked, with astonished eyes, at the man who suddenly stood there in the doorframe turning dead white.

It's all over, Nico thought. He understood that he had done something stupid that could never be made right again. He staggered and shut his eyes. His body fell lightly against the side of the half-open door. When he opened his eyes again, the woman still stood two steps away from him in the hallway. Her suffering face now wore an understanding smile, which also made it possible to see the gaps in her teeth. Nico put the index finger of his right hand to his mouth, nodded slowly and sadly at her with his contorted face, and gently shut the door.

The woman went to the next door and put the laundry bag down in the bedroom. When she climbed back down the stairs, Nico lay wet with sweat on his bed, as though paralyzed, his face covered with both hands. He no longer knew if the encounter had been real or just a dream. His head ached.

A little later, Marie came and brought tea. There was a knock on the door; he opened it, but he stayed hidden behind the door and only held out his hand to her. Then he quickly shut the door again. Marie went away without suspecting a thing.

The rest of the afternoon was a long wait that almost shredded his nerves to pieces. Would Marie come? What would she say? What excuse could he give? Nothing, nothing, he had betrayed himself. It was all over. He had to leave here, change his hiding place. But where would he go? Where?

But Marie didn't come until she brought him downstairs for dinner.

He was pale and distraught. No matter how hard he tried to act like everything was normal, he could not manage to answer Wim's hello with the same ease and natural tone. Wim and Marie both noticed it right away and left him alone. They knew he had moods like this sometimes, moods that rose up now and then and disappeared again, like thunderstorms that couldn't quite make it across a body of water. Poor devil! Who knew what thoughts oppressed him. The prospect of yet another winter? . . .

That evening he went back to his room early.

The woman had not said anything. Nico felt her silence as a double burden. It made it his duty to speak up, but he didn't say anything either. And for him it was a deception, almost a betrayal. He admitted it to himself. But still he kept quiet. Why? Out of fear of the consequences, which he did not know but which presented themselves as terrible in any case. They would turn him out of the house on the spot, or even . . . He knew that he was irrationally conjuring up a danger that would be easy to avert if they knew about it. But he kept quiet, with a grim stubbornness. It stayed a secret, and he held on to the foolhardy hope that it would continue to stay a secret.

Starting in December, the cleaning woman no longer appeared at the house. She stayed away on her own account. Her health had gotten worse again.

When Nico thought about her, the same cold terror ran through him as before and he shut his eyes. Later he felt a kind of longing for the gap-toothed smile on that suffering, puffy face, a craving that imperceptibly lessened his fear. He could not answer the question: Why?

VI.

Sometimes he had moments, hours of blind despair and dull hopelessness, when he hated them—them and the vase that stood downstairs in the front room, on a little table with a lace doily next to the bookcase. It was a Chinese vase, an acquisition of Wim's. He had brought it home from an auction one day, as a present for Marie and, he added laughing, for himself.

It was about sixteen inches high, porcelain, hand-painted with lustrous blue and red flowers and figures. Despite its size and its double-curved form it looked charming and delicate. It was their quiet pride and joy. They never needed to point it out to anyone; whoever walked into the room noticed it right away; Nico too when he saw it for the first time. He admired it unreservedly. Wim stood nearby and laughed, bashful and a little mischievous.

"But yes, it's a beautiful thing to have in your house . . . ! How did you find it?" Wim told the story:

". . . and I'd never been to a real auction before. It was really exciting! I saw it standing there before the auction started, and I just bid along with everyone else. To tell you the truth I couldn't afford it. It was like I was drunk."

"Yes, yes, I know how that is."

"You can't always be reasonable, you know? Marie's eyes almost popped out of her head at first. But she didn't say anything. And now . . . ! If we weren't in such times, we would have bought some more. We have a couple of books about Far Eastern art too. Right there . . . ," and he pointed to the second shelf of the bookcase.

"But why not? If you have the money, now is the best time to invest in something of lasting value."

Wim laughed. "Of course, but not vases. If something happens, they're the first thing to break in half."

"May I hold it for a moment?" Nico had asked.

"It's not heavy at all, just a little slippery."

And Nico had held it carefully in both hands while he gently turned it all the way around and examined it, attentively and lovingly. It was, in fact, a magnificent specimen, one to be truly proud of.

Then Wim had taken it back—"All right, give it here"—and put it down again on the small table, with one hand.

But in his downcast hours of deep despondency, Nico could have hurled down the vase too, shattered it to pieces, if it were here in his room. Since he couldn't touch it, all that remained was to hate it. It became a symbol to him: he hated this symbol, and he hated the people who owned this symbol.

Then his room was filled with suffering faces—contorted, disfigured, beaten to a pulp—whose features he eagerly studied to see if they weren't perhaps known to him. He heard groaning, whimpering, sniveling, wailing, calling upon God, cursing God; saw men and women, very old and very young—they were endless, the images he saw and heard in these hours. He lay on the sofa, fully clothed, and in his dazed state he was as if lying in wait for new images that washed up out of his imagination and brought with them new agitations and new, more painful images.

When he breathed in deep, he tasted gas. Gas! His room was full of gas! He closed his eyes and burrowed his head into the pillow. What did the others understand of all this? And if they did understand it—what did it mean to them? In their safe, protected, domestic life!—Safe? Protected? Since they had taken him in? No, no, he was being unfair. But their house, their home, their things—their world—how it all had attracted him and soothed him at first. And now: how vain, how inflated, how worthless! For he measured things now with a cosmic measure, which gripped him tight and shook him back and forth. What trust in each other? What danger? And what a gulf between people! Consolation! Consolation? . . . Was there any such thing?

When he stood at the window behind the curtain and looked out—"outside" was a mosaic of countless little squares and rectangles—it was better, sometimes. But other times, often, he didn't have the heart to stand up from the bed, to arise and venture the few steps to the window. He lay there as though in chains and brooded. Memories rose up inside him, and not only personal memories: history took shape, the past spoke the bloody language of fate. And horror, horror, overpowering, the way something is only when it rises up out of forgetting.

When he came here, to this house, he would have happily taken a place on a pile of coal in a barn and been satisfied. Now he slept in a bed, ate at a table, was treated as a human being.

But the longer it lasted, the greater his demands grew. Since he couldn't demand anything of the outer world—what he did receive was freely offered, almost a gift—his demands turned inward and more and more excessive. But people were helping him, they were helping him, didn't that mean anything? Yes, it meant a lot. And it was also nothing. He was turning into nothing. It was unbearable. It meant his annihilation, his human annihilation, even if it—maybe—saved his life. The little thorn that grows invisibly in anyone who lives on the help and pity of others grew to gigantic proportions, became a javelin lodged deep in his flesh and hurting terribly.

How proudly they had given him this room, how

gratefully he had received it. How imprisoned, abandoned, and wretched he had felt in it. The loneliness of loneliness. He had never liked to spend too much time at home, and now he had to. A spring arrived, a summer, an autumn . . . behind the curtains. The landscape, the sky, the distant sea, were not always a consolation, a balm to soothe the eye. Often, too often, they were a door that stayed closed.

With his counterfeit papers he could risk being out on the street during new moons in fall and winter. He went alone. They had precisely calculated the days in advance on the calendar, together. "So, Nico, from ———— to ———— you can go for a quiet little walk. No more than an hour, and not too far from the house. And don't come back to the house too late, because of the neighbors."

"Yes, thank you, Wim."

They shared his happiness. "At least you can stretch your legs. You'll still have to do without sunshine."

But he appeased them and said that even this little thing felt like a piece of good fortune.

Good fortune!— And still the constant fear that a flashlight would suddenly come on in the darkness before him and a stern voice would ask, while the light blinded his face: "Aha! So, ah . . . Where do you live?" He doesn't say anything. "Come on, tell me already." He stays stubbornly silent. "You'll tell me all right. Come with me." And he knows what that means. He will confess everything, yes, he will say everything . . . I live at . . . No, no, not that, that would be cowardice, villainy, they didn't deserve that. Even if they killed him, tortured him to death, he would keep his mouth shut, despite, yes, despite all their torture and . . . Marie, Wim, you can count on me, they'll get nothing out of me!

When he stood up from the family table that evening, he walked into the front room and stood for a long time in front of the vase, a few steps away from it. Finally he went up to it and pensively smoothed out a little crease in the lace doily it stood on.

VII.

MARIE WAS STILL STANDING IN THE KITCHEN DOING THE laundry when Wim appeared at her side. He made a noticeable fuss busying himself about the stove and the stone kitchen counter, where pots and bowls were standing that he shoved back and forth as though he were looking for something. He didn't find it, whatever it was. All the while he was sneaking a surreptitious look at Marie, who pulled a shirt out of the soapy water, looked at it, and then dunked it back in. No, she wasn't crying anymore. She seemed calmer to him. Her face was still red but that could just as well be from the effort and the steam.

"What are you looking for?" she asked, without looking up, and kept working. Laundry these days, when you couldn't get any decent detergent anymore . . . !

"Oh, never mind."

"Matches?"

"Yes, I thought they were here—"

"In the drawer on the right." She turned her head

without taking a break from her scrubbing. "No—there—yes. Aren't there any in the room?"

"I couldn't find them there either," Wim said. Then he saw them lying on the ledge by the stove, behind the photograph of his mother. He took the box and left again.

She hadn't asked, but the doctor must be coming back at any moment. Wim was growing impatient.

It was Nico's shirt that she had pushed back into the soapy water. She hadn't waited until Coba came; she herself started washing whatever clothes of his she could find.

He had brought only clothes with him; Marie had given him sheets and towels. She also darned his stockings and mended his suits. So much was falling apart, and he didn't have much. Most of the wash, and Wim's clothes, she took to a laundry.

During his illness he had gone through especially many clothes; she had to change the sheets three times, plus the washcloths, the pajamas. At first it was just an ordinary cold—stuffy nose, scratchy throat, a hacking cough every now and then. As so often happens when the seasons are changing. Nico had managed a few jokes about it at first. "My right tonsil," he said, and he seemed to swallow, his hand on his throat. "The right—you know, if you take the time to do it you can watch it yourself and see very nicely how it progresses. Tomorrow it'll be in the left one too"—again his hand on his throat, a painful swallow—"I feel it today already."

Marie had laughed too, even though she could tell how dejected and defeated he felt.

They treated it themselves, with aspirin, hot fluids, a scarf around his neck in the evenings. Wim had come home and told them how many people at his factory were out with the exact same symptoms. It is always a consolation to learn that something unpleasant is shared by everyone.

One evening he suddenly had a fever. Aspirin again, a bigger dose. When his temperature reached 102 they decided to fetch their doctor. Dr. Nelis, an even younger man, energetic, unmarried, understood right away what the situation was, even before Wim had brought him all the way into his confidence. He had several such cases in his practice at the moment.

"Doctor, there's one more thing . . ."

"The neighbors? I understand."

"It's that my wife . . . and I . . . They can see, of course, that we're still healthy and up and about . . ."

"What do you mean?" the doctor replied. "There are invisible illnesses too, that you can have and still be up and about."

"But they know that we've never been sick. And so if you start coming more often now . . . all at once like this . . ." He looked at the floor.

Silence. Dr. Nelis folded his hands and thought hard about it for a moment.

Suddenly he looked up and said, "Do you have a record player?"

"A record player?" Wim was absolutely staggered. What could a record player possibly have to do with it? "No!"

"Too bad."

Silence again.

"Maybe I could borrow one," Wim responded, without knowing why exactly he should borrow a record player. Neither of them was particularly musical, Marie and him.

"Really? Oh, never mind, we don't need it," the doctor said. But Wim noticed that the doctor was still thinking about this record player.

Finally he worked up the courage and asked, "Why, Doctor? Why a record player?"

Dr. Nelis smiled a little and looked fixedly at Wim.

"Oh"—the words came out of his mouth slowly and with a slight drawl, as though he were making a little fun of himself—"well, I'm crazy about records, I have quite a collection myself. It's my hobby. Everyone in town knows that about me—people know something like that about anyone who's even a little in the public eye, after all. I could say that I was visiting you to listen to one of your records. A particular record I've been trying to chase down forever and that you happen to have, 'L'invitation au Voyage' for example, with words by Baudelaire, music by—Duparc? or Poulenc? . . . which one is it again?"

"I have no idea," Wim answered. "I don't know it."

"Too bad," the doctor said, "it's heavenly—the vocals . . . *'Luxe, calme, volupté.'*" He hummed the melody softly. "I wish I owned it." He stared at the ceiling, lost in a reverie. "*Enfin*, I'll come to give your wife a couple of calcium injections against fatigue and general listlessness. There's a lot of that going around these days. Goodbye."

In the meantime, Marie had told Nico that Wim had gone for the doctor.

"Isn't it too risky—for you . . ." he had asked in a dull voice.

"Don't worry, Nico. Dr. Nelis is good, in every way. And you're sick."

"Yes, I do feel sick," he answered softly, and he leaned back deeper into the pillow and shut his eyes. He had always known that they wouldn't leave him in the lurch here . . .

"As long as it doesn't turn into a double pneumonia," Dr. Nelis said to Marie and Wim downstairs in the back room, after he had thoroughly examined the patient. "He isn't strong."

Marie turned pale. "I do what I can, with the food situation . . ."

"I know, it's impossible to manage," the doctor replied. "His inner defenses too are not that strong . . . at least that's how it seems to me. And no wonder!" he added. "I gave him an injection. I'll come again tonight."

After a week his condition was unchanged, despite

the new medicine that everyone was talking about at the time.

Marie was gripped by an uneasiness she had never felt before. She suffered. It wasn't so much the thought that he might not get through his illness, it was the idea that his defenses weren't strong enough. What could she do?

When he was still healthy and stuck in his room, in recent days and weeks, she had never forgotten to put on a happy and confident face when she walked in. She had read somewhere or other, in a housewives' magazine that was still appearing at irregular intervals, that you had to stay positive. Positive! That was supposed to be the best way to overcome difficult circumstances. Without her exactly realizing it, this thought had lodged deep inside her and revealed itself first through her attitude toward Nico. Stay positive! But after he fell sick, it didn't seem to work for her anymore. Carefully, timidly, she crept into his room and watched his feverish, sweaty face with its closed eyes and half-open mouth struggling for breath. In his illness and helplessness, his whole being—or at least so she felt—expressed itself more clearly, and she had never perceived it more deeply than she did now. Sick and helpless, wasn't this his true state? His behavior before was what was remarkable: playing chess—with himself—practicing French and English, reading books. All of it, all of it, was nothing but a kind of medicine to try to heal his affliction. And Wim and she had often wondered at his behavior. Sometimes it seemed to her almost uncanny. It stood like a wall between him and them, which slowly, slowly crumbled as the war dragged on and everything aberrant and inhuman became typical and everyday.

"I have to go look in on him again," she said one night after she and Wim had gone to bed.

"He's probably already asleep—you'll wake him up . . ."

She insisted: "I'll be very quiet."

Even before she had finished closing the door to his room behind her, she heard a breathless, congested voice: "Marie . . ."

She turned on the light; the bed stood outside its dim circle of illumination. His beard had grown and it covered his chin and cheeks, so that he looked older and more emaciated. She stood next to his bed.

"Should I fluff the pillow for you again?"

"Ah, yes."

She helped him sit up. He supported himself with great difficulty on the mattress while she hurriedly pounded the pillow with both hands. It was limp with heat. Then she helped him as he let himself fall back. It visibly did him good. His hair was a confused tangle on his head, like the absolute mess after a downpour. It hung damp and sticky over his forehead and temples. The half darkness of the room gave his face an ashy coloring. Two feverish eyes were wide-open in his face, as though gathering all the shadows of the bedroom into themselves.

"Marie . . ."

"Yes?" She spoke very softly as though afraid to make his condition worse with any loud noise. But he didn't say anything else. He closed his eyes and lay there as though he had just that moment fallen asleep. Only his arms, stretched out on the blanket but lying right up against his body, trembled now and then. Then he raised them gingerly, straight up, and let them fall again, like wings that he wanted to unfold but then, tired and powerless, just curled up again. It was almost as if he were not breathing anymore. Only the blanket on his body moved, almost imperceptibly, up and down.

Marie bent down over his stubbly face so that she could pick up the softest sound from his lips in case he looked like he was about to speak. She waited like that for a time. She saw the beads of sweat on his forehead and the little rivulets slowly dripping down his face and neck and sinking into the cavities above his collarbone. His pajama top was half open, and a warm, strong smell rose up toward her from the damp shining skin under the hair on his chest. When she felt under his armpits, she noticed that the fabric was soaked through with sweat, the fabric at his sides and his elbows too.

She took a washcloth and first wiped his face and head; then, after opening another button of his pajama top, she washed his chest and painstakingly wiped his armpits. She felt the heat from his body. She fetched a bottle of eau de cologne from her bedroom, a bottle she had saved for special occasions, sprayed a few drops onto his forehead, and blew on it lightly to spread the perfume so that its coolness would pleasantly refresh his hot skin. It helped. She saw his face become more lively again.

"I'll get you a fresh pair of pajamas, yes?" she said, bent closely over him.

A weak nod was the answer. When she was going over to the hiding place where his clothes were, she heard him say, with great effort, "I don't have any more . . ."

He didn't own much, and what little he had had been used up in the days he'd been sick. She went out to the hall, where the laundry bag was still full of the clean clothes that had come back from the laundry that day, and she pulled out a pair of Wim's pajamas from the bottom of the bag. She called Wim to come help her, and together they dressed Nico. Even though he couldn't do much to help, since he was already so weakened by his illness, and even though they themselves had no experience nursing sick people, everything went smoothly.

"Thank you, it was so hot," he said weakly, when he was lying motionless on his back again. Wim was already in the doorway.

"So, you'll sleep better now. Good night," Marie said, and she left the room on tiptoes.

Outside in the hall, they stopped for a moment and listened, as though standing outside a room where a child was sleeping. Their eyes met.

"Come on, Marie!" He opened the door to their room.

She followed slowly after him, still on tiptoes.

VIII.

THE DOCTOR WAS STANDING IN THE FRONT HALL IN HIS hat and coat. It was quarter past ten. He rubbed his hands together. "I came on my bicycle," he said. He usually used a motorcycle, since he'd had to put his car into a garage because of the shortage of gasoline. It was pitch-black outside. "We're going right now?" he asked, and he peered up the steps.

Marie had taken off her apron. Her hands were puffy and red, her face was shining. Still, she was calm and focused. "Can I help with something," she said, "or . . ."

"Let's go," Wim said to the doctor, and let him go first. Then, turning back to Marie, "It's better if you wait here downstairs, maybe in the front room . . ."

"Don't forget the coat," she replied.

Wim stopped on the stairs. "Right," he said, and he leaped back down in two big jumps. He pulled his hat down tight over his head.

"Which door?" the doctor asked when Wim came running back up the stairs behind him. He was a little out of breath because he was wearing his heavy winter coat.

They walked into the room in their hats and coats like two men from some commission, officials who had come to launch an investigation into a case of death where foul play was suspected. They stepped decisively up to the bed, stood standing alongside it for a second, and calmly considered the case before them, their hands buried deep in their coat pockets. Then the doctor shoved his left hand under the dead man's neck, grabbed his stiff left arm with the other hand, and pulled. The body slid out of the symmetrical position it had been in until then, and now lay a little diagonal and tilted onto the right side of the face and body. The doctor looked at the prominent Adam's apple of the dead man in silence. Wim stood hesitantly next to him.

"If we sit him up first," he said.

"That won't work," the doctor answered, puffing up his cheeks a little, "with the rigor mortis." He had already tested it out. Silence. Wim held his hands clasped behind his back; he had the strange feeling of not being in his own house, but rather in a strange house for a wake.

"It's not so simple, really," the doctor began anew.

Wim turned back the covers and measured the length of the body. "It seems to me, Doctor—like this— if we lay him across our shoulders, like a plank, I could maybe do it myself . . ."

"Impossible! You think with a dead body . . . !"

"Or I could have him on my back, piggyback, and you could prop him up from behind so that he doesn't fall backward"—and he lightly bent forward and pulled the arms into two curves at chest height, as though putting them into two stirrups—"like this."

The doctor hesitated before he answered: "The joints are still too stiff."

Wim was silent.

"Have you ever actually seen a corpse?" the doctor asked suddenly, and turned the body onto its back. Wim gave a start.

"Of course," he said hastily, "my father, a long time ago, I was very young."

"I see." And then he went on, staring at the blankets: "I am always surprised how few grown men and women have actually really seen a dead body. That is, in normal times. A lot of people see one for the first time in their thirties. It's strange. Everyone has a lot more to do with love, earlier and more often, of course. But they should have to see a dead body at least once a week. Then everyone would have a better sense of equilibrium, and lots of fears and anxieties would just disappear." He pulled his gaze back from the blankets and raised it to Wim. "Do you still remember it, then?"

"Sure I do," Wim answered, and reflected back, thinking hard.

He was a boy, seven years old, when one day—he

was wearing a black velvet coat with a cream-colored pointed collar—his mother called him into the music room, where there was an open coffin. She herself was standing, with tear-swollen eyes, in a posture that he would never forget, tall and straight with her thin figure, as though she were growing from one minute to the next, leaning against one of the double doors and saying in a soft, melodious voice—she was a singer—and a tone he had never heard her speak in before and would never hear again: "Wim, that's Father. He is dead. Say goodbye to him, my boy." And Wim had stepped up to the open coffin, which had a long piece of glass lying across the top, lengthwise, and had looked closely at Father. What was that under his chin? A long, wide block of wood lay on his chest and held up Father's chin. His face looked serious and was almost totally without wrinkles. He looked different, better than he did before when he was lying sick in bed. He was wearing a frock coat with a big white carnation from the garden in the buttonhole. Wim examined the carnation and noticed that you can't smell a flower through glass. Only in this flower, blooming behind glass but giving off no more scent, did the astonished child recognize the sign of death. His father also lay behind the glass covering and you could see him but not smell him. Two thick, burning candles stood at the head end of the coffin, and at the foot end lay a big wreath with a blue ribbon, on which was written in golden letters: TO THEIR BELOVED DADDY — THE CHILDREN.

"He's still too young," his aunt whispered to his mother when she saw the boy standing there.

"Thank God," his uncle whispered back. Father's brother had been living in the house for a week and taking care of all the necessary business. The following year, he married Wim's mother and moved to India with her. The children were sent to boarding school.

When Wim's aunt led him quietly out of the room, Coba came in through the other door. She was very pale and sobbing uninterruptedly. Even though she was older, the rules of family precedence demanded that the son take his leave of his father first . . .

"The two of us will manage it." The doctor interrupted the silence.

"Yes," Wim answered with conviction, as though he had had the exact same thought at the same time. How yellow Nico's teeth looked already, like wax. Were they cold to the touch too?

"Grab his feet," the doctor said as he gripped under the armpits and lifted the upper body from the sheets. They laid him on the floor. Then they started over, their faces turned toward each other, Wim at the foot end and the doctor at the head end, and they carried the corpse by the armpits and feet, the way it was done in old "Burial of Christ" paintings, slowly and carefully—Wim was walking backward—out of the bedroom and down the stairs.

The light was on in the stairwell. When they opened the door, they would be visible from outside.

"Let's put him down again," the doctor said. He seemed uncomfortable carrying the body this way.

"Here in the hall?" Wim replied, and laid the legs down on the carpet. Something inside him resisted the idea of laying the dead body right down here in the hallway, where everybody walked back and forth all the time.

The doctor straightened up, since he had been bent over the whole time they were carrying the body. "A sheet—we need some kind of sheet to wrap him up," he said. "The pajamas will be too bright outside."

"Marie, get a sheet, or a blanket," Wim said after opening the door to the room where Marie sat waiting with nothing to do. "We need to wrap him in something dark."

"A blanket?" She stood up quickly and hurried from the room. She had been staring at the clock the whole time; it was after 10:30 and there was no time to lose if Wim was to get home again before curfew. He wanted to call after her that he would get the blanket himself, if she would only tell him where . . . But she was already out of the room.

She was not prepared to see him again, here in the hall and lying on the floor in such a position. She had no doubt heard the men slowly, step by step, coming down the stairs with a heavy weight. But still, catching sight of him like this came as quite a shock. There, where the milk bottles and bread basket and all the other everyday things stood during the day, where the letters fell when they were slipped through the mail slot, where you walked in and out, and where he himself had come in— there he lay now, dead. The doctor was standing on the stairs, his right elbow propped on the banister and his head in the palm of his hand. In front of him, on the floor between the stairs and the door to the front room: the body.

Since she had left the front room at full speed and shut the door behind her, she had no other choice, her feet acted on their own, defending themselves as though she were suddenly standing in front of an abyss, taking a couple of tiny steps and then jumping over Nico with a little leap, a small, barely noticeable jump, just enough to clear the body. Her eyes, reflecting horror, shame, and sadness, were looking at the doctor, who was watching this performance—first her hesitation and then her helpless decision—without changing his position, bent over with his head in his hand. He nodded to her. "And some safety pins too," he whispered, "please—"

"Of course," she breathed, and crept sideways up the stairs.

The three of them wound the body in a blanket that had earlier been on his bed, and fastened the bundle with pins as though preparing him for a sailor's grave. When they were done, the clock in the hall showed ten minutes to eleven. In ten minutes they could have all this behind them.

Marie turned out the light in the hall and opened the house door.

The moonless night was cold. Marie shivered. It's good that he's snugly wrapped in a warm blanket, she thought, and this curious idea wouldn't let her go even though she realized in the same moment that whether it was cold or warm he wouldn't feel anything. Nico, Nico . . .

The men in their coats stared out into the shapeless, chilly darkness and listened tensely for any sound. A house door banged shut a little farther up the street. There was a whistle. A dog came bounding with muffled, flying leaps across the gravel, shooting through the night. Silence.

"Let's go," Wim ordered softly, and he grabbed the legs from the floor with both hands, bundling them together, and lifted them onto his right hip so that he could walk forward this time, even if he did have to walk turned slightly to the right. At the same time, the doctor pulled the shrouded body up from the ground in one motion and supported it on his right shoulder, wrapping both arms tightly around it.

The first steps down the garden path to the gate and down the sidewalk were hurried and bumpy as the dead body pitched from side to side. They had trouble keeping it from slipping out of their hands. By the time they got to the street they had found their rhythm, or it had found itself, and the body moved back and forth with it, making it easier for them to carry it. They cautiously crept through the darkness and stepped softly so that no one would hear them. Only a few feet on the other sidewalk, and then they would have to turn into the park entrance. Wim, who went first, felt more than saw where the chain-link fence separating the footpath from the park was interrupted by an opening. The doctor, who was carrying the greater burden, willingly followed.

Here at the entrance to the park, shielded by bushes whose tops cast weak black shapes against the darkness, they felt safer. Thanks to the rain of the past few days, the ground was loose enough to muffle their footsteps, but also not so wet that they would get stuck. After a few hundred feet they crossed over the high arch of a narrow wooden bridge, under which a little waterway flowed through the park and ended in a small pond surrounded by poplars and lindens, right at the edge of the pastures and fields. The planks creaked and they hurried to get back to the path. On the other side, twenty feet away, stood a gnarled, formless mass, black in the darkness. It was a bench—two flat, horizontal planks with a gap in between as the sitting surface and a sharply tilted plank in parallel as a back support, with feet and joints of cast iron.

After they put the blanket onto the bench and rolled out the body, they lifted it over the back of the backrest, put it down on the edge of the grass, and pushed it carefully between the cast-iron feet. It fit comfortably. Then they took the same way back, in silence, a tired, numb feeling in their arms. It struck eleven. Three minutes later the doctor got on his bicycle in front of the house. Since Wim didn't know if he should thank the doctor or not, he only whispered, "Good night."

"Good night," Dr. Nelis murmured, and disappeared into the darkness. Wim went into the house.

After he had taken off his hat and coat, he stood for a moment—as he never usually did—in front of the little oval mirror in the hall. He straightened his tie, wiped his forehead and between his neck and collar with a hand-kerchief, combed his hair, and did similar things that you think of only when you're in front of a mirror. He was amazed and found it hard to grasp that he looked the way his mirror image showed him.

Marie hurried down the stairs. She looked pale, with a touching tension around her mouth and eyes. Doubt-less she had been crying upstairs in his bedroom.

"So," Wim said, looking straight at her a little pity-ingly.

She didn't ask anything. He pressed his lips together and nodded a couple times, as if to say: So, we managed it . . .

They went into the back room. Wim fell into the armchair next to the stove, his legs crossed, his hands spread wide, gripping the arms of the chair as though he wanted to jump right up again.

Marie sat at the table.

Silence. She waited like someone who herself had something to hide. Should she go first?

"The stove is off," Wim said. He stroked its cold iron with his hand.

Would it be better for her to tell him now, after all? It was ultimately nothing very important . . . It was so cold down here.

"I'll brew us up some coffee," Marie said, and stood up hastily.

Us? The two of them, Wim and herself. And a dry ship's biscuit along with it, as always.

While they were drinking their coffee, Wim suddenly stretched and asked, "Is it raining?"

They both listened.

"No—thank God, no." Pause.

The three of them had ended every single day like this for almost a year, together, with a cup of coffee and a dry piece of hardtack, often in silence, each given over to their thoughts, but still together—waiting, waiting . . . There was gratitude in this habit, and a little tiredness, from the night to come that they were about to enter alone or as a pair, and a furtive, sad happiness in the smiling, incomprehensible futility.

. . . He fit comfortably underneath, Wim eventually thought.

"Did you bring back the blanket?" Marie asked timidly.

"Outside in the hall."

It got colder in the room. And so empty . . .

Why didn't Wim say anything? Had he maybe noticed something after all? Should she go first and tell him—oh, it was too insignificant. But it had struck her a blow, this last thing, this revelation, this last, unheard conversation. Tomorrow, maybe, she would be able to tell him.

"Let's go to sleep, Marie," Wim said. He started his nightly tour through the house, part of the regular duties of a proper man of the house before going to sleep: front door, door to the shed, back door, all closed, the gas in the kitchen turned off, wood chopped in the cellar for the next morning. In the last few months he had also gone upstairs to check that the windows were closed there too. You never knew . . . Today too he went upstairs. Actually it's pointless, he said to himself.

But he did it anyway. You don't unlearn an old, year-long habit as quickly as that.

IX.

"AS LONG AS IT DOESN'T RAIN!" MARIE TOSSED AND turned—as she had many times already—onto her right side, pulled up her knees, and listened into the night . . . As long as it doesn't rain. He should at least be spared that.

She could not get warm. Wim lay next to her in his bed, the blanket pulled up over his head, and he slept. No noise came from outside. Only the warm, muffled beating of his breath against the blanket, next to her, slow and heavy, as though he had to sleep against a certain resistance.

The first night Nico was in the house, she had also not been able to sleep, more from fear and amazement: whether it would all turn out well, and that no one had discovered him yet. Back then at the beginning, everything in the house had seemed so different to her, every slight sound had suddenly taken on a new meaning through the secret that she was hiding under her roof.

A secret! It was not only that they had sheltered him—he himself, his person, his life, constituted the secret. It was as though a no-man's-land lay all around him, alien and impenetrable. It was impossible to bridge the gap. Even while he was alive, everything she heard him say, everything she saw—his voice, his movements—was like something seen from the opposite bank of a river while mist hung over the water and masked any clear view. It almost melted away into the impersonal, colorless swirls of fog. Now he was dead and they had managed to get him out of the house—but a secret had been left behind, as one last thing. At first it seemed to her that she, tears in her eyes and alone in his room, had discovered it, as though the fog had suddenly lifted and the other riverbank had come closer, right up next to her, so that she could see it precisely and know everything about it: its slope, its bushes and shrubs and hollows. Yet the more she looked, the more it rose like mist from the water, enveloping everything. Marie was frightened when she realized that a secret you discover by chance only conceals another, still greater secret behind it, which can never be discovered. And that every bit of knowledge, every revelation, is only like egg whites whisked until they're sweet and mixed into the dough to break it up and release its flavor . . .

She was itching to tell Wim about it; best would be now, while it was still close to her. When he woke up, she would start. Should she wake him up?

Marie straightened up, dug her elbows into the soft pillow, and supported her head in her hands. Next to her was the hidden, muffled beating of a warm body. It was so cold tonight! She pulled the blankets up over her shoulders and back. Again she saw the picture before her eyes.

After she had carefully shut the house door behind the two men, she had run quickly up to his room. She could still hear the footsteps hurriedly and unsteadily moving farther and farther away on the gravel. Then it was quiet. She looked around the room and began straightening up. Not so much out of fear that when they found him someone might come here, where he had hidden, nor from a desire to remove all his traces, as out of a secret wish to have him near her again. The men carried the body; she too could carry something—his things, what he had lived with.

She had always taken care to keep his room so that, if necessary, just a quick tidying up would make it look uninhabited. His suits and coat stayed in Wim's closet; his clothes, writing implements, papers, and toiletries remained concealed in the hiding place.

Once, on a Sunday, the doorbell rang and an older man, a stranger, asked to speak to Wim. Marie let him into the front hall and asked, just in passing, what matter this might be concerning.

"Are you the woman of the house?" the stranger replied, and he looked at Marie with what seemed to her a peculiar, rather pointed smile. It made her uneasy. When she said yes, he hesitated a moment before saying, "Well, I'd much rather discuss it with your husband, confidentially." Confidentially! Marie was terribly afraid. This didn't sound good.

She called Wim and then hurried upstairs. "Nico, a strange man . . . Come on, disappear." She helped him stuff his things into a small valise that stood prepared for cases like this, and opened the closet. The hiding place was behind it. They had come across it by accident.

Between the two rooms on the second floor ran the stairs to the first floor. If you took out the side wall of the built-in closet in Nico's room, on the side where the stairs were, you found an empty space roomy enough to hide someone. Wim, in his spare time, had cleanly sawed off the bottom half of the wooden wall, put in molding to conceal the signs of the sawing, and run the molding around the entire closet, halfway up, to give a uniform impression. On the bottom too, where the wall met the floor, he had added a baseboard for support. With one skillful hand movement, which Nico soon practiced and mastered, you could take out the wall, slip inside, and fasten the wall from the inside with bolts and crossbars while someone put the wall back in place from the outside. It was good work, well made, and they had all taken pleasure in it.

The strange man stayed a bit longer than half an hour—he had come on someone's recommendation and was looking for a place to house someone who had gone into hiding. Wim had to bring all his cleverness to bear, to decline in a circumspect way without letting it show that they already had someone: "It's just that we've been married such a short time, you understand, and we're much too careless and inexperienced with such things, especially my wife, no, no, and I'm gone all day too." Even when someone came recommended, you had to be careful. It might be a provocateur trying to get into your confidence . . .

—Well, Nico stayed the whole time like a scared little sheep in his pen and waited until they let him out again. Luckily such visits didn't happen often.

Marie pulled the sheet off the bed. By now they must be turning into the park. No, this was not the ending they expected. They had imagined it differently—not ending for them until it all ended. How, exactly? Maybe that she and Wim would one day appear upstairs and tell him: "Nico, we made it!"? Or in the middle of the night, the thunder of the artillery from the coast, the indescribable din of thousands of airplanes, bombs, and the delicate, rhythmical clattering of the machine guns? . . . And he, yes, what would he do? What would he have done . . . Cheer? Hug them? Marie! Wim! It's happened, at last, too late but at last—at last! Or, in a weak voice, half questioning, as though he couldn't quite believe it: "Really?" He would look at her hopelessly, his eyes filled with tears, as if he were in shock. "But Nico, aren't you happy?" Yes, of course, but still, could you call this happiness? He had grown so tired from the long wait, from being shut away. His happiness too had grown so tired, so locked away . . . What would he actually do? She had often thought about it. But in truth it was impossible to imagine.

She lifted out the wall and took the things from the hiding place: the little laundry bag, a few stockings, a folder with a pen, books. When she pulled out a few newspapers that he had saved, God knows why, a little packet fell to the floor. She bent down. What was that? It was a tiny little bundle of sealed yellow paper, half opened on one corner, LUCKY STAR printed in big black letters. A pinch of tobacco fell out and scattered on the floor. Cigarettes! American cigarettes! She smelled them. Delicate, spicy American tobacco, the kind she had smoked before the war and not since, not for years. How did he get a hold of this packet? From Coba? Or had he saved it as a kind of relic? Why? And hidden it from them here in the hiding place? It was still more than half full, he had smoked maybe six or seven. Smoked them alone! Wim too, he would have so loved to . . . But he smoked them alone!

And suddenly she had understood, fully understood. She saw it in front of her. She felt an ache, a constriction in her throat, which had gone dry, and without realizing it tears came to her eyes. She sat down on the couch, the packet still in her hand. Smoked them alone! Smoked when he was alone—when he felt lonely—when he couldn't go on . . . He hid it from them!

She saw him lying here on the couch, staring at the blanket. His left arm curled under his head on the pillow, his right hand on his forehead. Nothing about him moves. Only when he breathes, a quaking and trembling fractures the flow of air into countless little clipped puffs of breath . . . I can't go on, I can't! But no screams, no rage, no tears. He stretches out his arms alongside his body and leaves them lying there, two worn-out, rotten wooden hooks. His breath gets shallower; there is no more quaking. His heart in his chest beats slowly, slowly; there's time, lots of time . . . Then he turns his head a little to the right and shuts his eyes. He is taken up into a kind of fog, his body gradually sucked into a whirlpool, limb by limb, casting up spray. But he doesn't feel any bliss, any salvation, any relief from the approaching annihilation . . . can't go on . . . can't go on. He lies there like that for a long time. Then all at once he sees himself lying there, as if in a mirror. He is frightened. He is lying across from himself; he could stretch out his hand and touch his own body over there. But no, at the same time he is immeasurably far removed from himself. And this combination, near and at the same time separate, awakens a feeling of tension, of torment, that takes away all his senses. There is nothing around him. Only him, alone, cut off from everything that is usually his, everything that binds him as with fine, thin nerve fibers to life itself.

Something in him arises, something in him has had

an idea. Still numb, he slowly gets up and slips like a sleepwalker to the closet, opens up the hiding place, rummages around, and finds the little yellow packet. It is still bulging, still full. He pulls out a cigarette and puts the rest back into the hiding place.

And then, on the edge of the couch, he smokes this cigarette, pull by pull . . .

When he has smoked it down to the end, he carries the ashtray with the stub to the garbage and empties it there. With his hand he waves away the faint smell of smoke in the room. No one needs to know . . .

A secret! No one needs to know, Marie thought, and shut her eyes, half upright in her bed. A wistful, melancholy feeling rises up in her, the same as the previous night in his room. Poor Nico! A secret—what a horrific piece of theater—from them, the ones who were keeping him as a secret. But had it never occurred to them that he too might have something he didn't share with them? Had they really forgotten? Were they without any secrets from him, for that matter? Sometimes they seemed to sense it, when they observed him without his realizing it, when he ate or sat there in silence and stared into space . . . Was it his race, the history of his people? Yes, that too, why deny it, but that was only part of it. For that was something they could understand to a certain extent, they could empathize and so share it with him somehow. Something different, foreign, something we ourselves are not, is relatively accessible to our understanding. But the decisive thing remains unexplained. The spark in him, the splinter of the great fire that burns in the world and that we call Life, mysterious, solitary, finding new form in every human being and revealing itself only in a fraction of a second, breaking through the fire wall of the body in an illuminated moment, and then a light, a sign of connection, of togetherness, but still solitary and indestructibly full of mystery.

The cigarettes belonged to him alone. Everything else he had shared with them, or they with him, depending on how you looked at it. He had often given her flowers, through Wim since he couldn't get them himself, and Wim got a little book as a present from him on his birthday. But the cigarettes—no, he couldn't share those.

What would Wim say? Would he understand, or would he be annoyed? He so craved a good cigarette.

Marie threw herself back onto the pillow and pulled the covers up under her chin. Wim still lay there with the covers over his head, his breath coming deep, heavy, and even. The poor boy, the whole experience hit him too, harder than he let on. Sleep was his only escape, the only way he could be fresh for work again in the morning. The excitement of the past few days had taken a lot out of him.

Nico was lying under a bench in the park. In just a few hours someone would find him. And then? Sometimes a quiet fear came over her, a fear that further complications were still to come. But she fought against it, she didn't want this fear. Should she tell Wim about it at all? Maybe tomorrow?

She dropped off to sleep. When she woke up again, she crept to the window and let a little air in through the blackout curtains. It was still night out. She lay down again but no longer felt tired. The experiences of last night were before her spirit again, but clearer, sharper, as though purified of all superficial thoughts and feelings through the fine-mesh sieve of sleep.

She felt connected to the dead man in a way she had never managed with the living. Outside, a cock crowed in a yard that bordered the park.

She would keep his secret, burn the cigarettes. No one else would ever smoke them!

X.

THE NEXT MORNING.

At first neither of them dared to look at each other.

"Good morning, Marie." —Slowly it changed.

Then, when they sat down together as usual at the breakfast table, which held as always the deep soup plates, bread, butter, and marmalade, they would have gladly discussed the situation again, especially what the future had in store. For they had, each of them in private, the uncertain feeling that it wasn't entirely played out yet. On the contrary. Something new could still follow, something they couldn't yet guess.

Even though they knew that they were both thinking the same thing, neither one dared to disturb the other's inner silence. Marie had put the pot of porridge back on the warm stove and now they both sat bent over the steaming plates and stirred the hot porridge. Now and then Wim paused from spooning his food, turned around in his chair, and started moving a poker back and forth in the stove, stirring around in the flame.

"Nice and warm," he said, and he rubbed his hands together.

"Do you want some more porridge?" Marie asked, and she stood up to take the pot from the stovetop.

"Why?" Wim asked. He ordinarily ate only one plateful.

"I had some extra milk," she answered.

"Ah, right."

She scooped some out for him and then took some more herself. Each of them ate one and a half portions.

"Do you want to maybe lie down again for a while?" Wim said, sticking his napkin back into the napkin ring. She looked like she had had a terrible night's sleep.

"Me? Why?" She looked at him questioningly. Had he observed her in the night after all? "You should have another piece of bread," she said. "You usually eat more anyway." Every morning, after their porridge, they ate two pieces of buttered toast with marmalade or another kind of spread.

"No thanks, I've had enough." He stayed calmly sitting in his chair, to keep her company.

"Then I'll give it to you for the office," she replied, and started cutting the bread . . . "You're coming home for lunch?" Because it sometimes happened that he stayed in the factory and took his midday meal with him in the morning.

"Of course—I'm coming home today . . ."

Finally she got up the courage.

"Do you think that we'll hear what . . . happened soon?"

"Definitely. Maybe as early as tomorrow."

"Tomorrow? So long?"

Pause.

She had put the last bite into her mouth, and as she put the cover on the butter dish and tightened the lid of the marmalade jar, tasks that seemed to require her whole attention, she got to the point: "Do you think there will be any complications?"

"Complications?" He thought about it. "No, I'm sure there won't be," he replied after a while, totally calm and in a tone meant to indicate how slight he thought the possibility was.

"But . . ."

"But? Oh, I don't think they'll go door-to-door searching houses over this."

His head tilted a little to one side—he considered. They hadn't, when you came right down to it, fully thought through all the consequences of the situation. They hadn't, and the doctor hadn't either. The only thought on their minds was to get the dead body out of the house as quickly as possible.

"But Wim!" Marie was slightly startled when he said "door-to-door." Even though she had secretly considered the possibility herself, it gave her a little shock to hear the words spoken. She made an effort to keep her thoughts in check and not give free rein to another feeling rising within her, a feeling of anxiety and fear.

He stood up. "If anything happens, you can reach me at the factory. I have to go now."

"See you later." In a sudden burst she threw her arms around him and kissed him. And when he kissed her back, he felt all at once how well she was holding up, how well she had held up all year.

"Don't worry about it," he said tenderly, "everything will be fine." At the moment when he said it, he believed it himself.

At half past nine the milkman came. He rang twice, one ring right after the other. Marie had worked out this signal with him and also with a few other people; it was nicer to know in advance whether there would be a known face or an unknown face on the other side of the door, in these times . . .

"Same as always," Marie said, and she passed him the blue enamel pot. He filled it up.

"They found a man here in the park this morning," he said, giving her back the filled pot. The sturdy kid stood there in his wooden shoes, legs wide apart, and he shut the lid on the white-enameled, thick-necked milk canister.

"So . . ." Marie replied. She couldn't see his face. Her heart began to pound but she stayed standing calmly in the door. "Any yogurt today?"

Without answering, he dragged the milk canister back to the street, lifted it onto his cart with one swing, and reappeared next to her with two little white bottles full of yogurt.

"Thanks."

"A dead man—" he continued.

"Here . . . in our park?" Marie asked, and she heard something else start to sound in her voice, a feeling of relief, of resolution . . . "Where did you hear that?" Did this question go too far? It suddenly struck her that he was offering up the same sensational piece of news from one house to the next, like a town crier, wherever his cart took him . . . They found a man here in the park this morning . . . A dead man! . . . Yes . . .

She had to laugh to herself, and something inside her made her want to keep going and finish the conversation with the milkman in a natural, genuine way.

"At six-thirty," he went on, "Melker saw it, biking in from the fields."

"So—what kind of man was it?" She held her breath, waiting for the answer.

"That I don't know," the milkman said, sticking both hands contemplatively into his pants pockets. His face grew serious, his lower lip protruding a little. "Some poor devil—sometimes you read it in the paper, too, that they found someone, on the road or wherever . . ." And then, in a soft voice, cautiously, "It'll probably turn out to have been a Jew . . ."

Pause.

"Oh, I see," Marie responded slowly, as though a light were dawning on her. "You mean . . . yes, it could be." She held the bottles tight against her body with her left arm, and the milk pot stood on the floor in the doorway to the house. She was still waiting. And . . . ?

A few houses down, a woman came out the door and through the front garden, milk pot in her hand. "Milkman!" she cried in a trilling falsetto voice, before she caught sight of him standing and talking with Marie in front of the house. With little nervous steps she hurried up to the cart he had left standing on the edge of the sidewalk. She held her milk pot up in the air and waved.

"Coming," the milkman called back, and he stayed, hands in his pockets, without moving from his place. And, turned to Marie: "She's in quite a hurry."

"Maybe," Marie replied. She had learned what she wanted to know—and another customer was already waiting at the milk cart. She could make it quick now, then disappear.

"Well . . . he couldn't have been with her, in any case," the milkman said, very softly, so that Marie could barely hear it.

She understood right away. Nevertheless she asked, innocently: "Who?"

"Well—" He waggled a big thumb quickly a few times back in the direction of the park.

"Why not?" Marie said, and a significant smile ended the sentence, as though she knew all sorts of secrets . . .

"Her?" the man whispered, and he took his left hand out of his pocket and bent closer to Marie. "She's much too scared." And his soft voice said everything he felt in that moment, his little contempt and mockery. And a laugh too, as though he knew still other secrets . . .

But he didn't really know them, he couldn't know them, Marie decided when she was alone in the house again. He was only trying to get across that he knew his clients. Of course it was easy to tell whether someone you sold milk to was acting scared, or more scared than usual. But still, it was eerie. She felt a little strange about it.

But Nico wasn't lying under the bench anymore! She could have screamed out loud when she heard the news, screamed for joy. This feeling of satisfaction suddenly rising within her—that he wasn't lying in the park anymore, under the sky, like a dead bird—it had given her the courage to conduct this conversation with the milkman to the end, in a rather daring and dangerous way. Eventually every house near the park would come under suspicion. Of course. She hadn't thought of that before.

When she stood in the kitchen again and put the bottles of milk and yogurt on the cold stone ledge, she knew at last that Nico had stopped living in her house. In her grief at his death, which broke through fully for the first time now that her fear was gone, there was mixed in a feeling of happiness, of satisfaction, that someone had found him and that nothing more could happen to him now. They would be alone again within the four walls of their house, just like before. Maybe a new guest would come but he, Nico, would never be standing at the top of the stairs again, waiting for someone to bring him his newspaper. He would never have to wait for anything again. He had defended himself against death from without, and then it had carried him off from within. It was like a comedy where you expect the hero to emerge onstage, bringing resolution, from the right. And out he comes from the left. Later, though, the audience members go home surprised, delighted, and a little bit wiser for the experience. They feel that the play did turn out a bit sad after all, at the very end. We thought he would enter from the right . . .

And then there was also a little embarrassment, a little disappointment. Why did he of all people have to die? Why did precisely the one who was hiding in their house have to die a perfectly ordinary, normal death, the same way people die all the time, whether in wartime or peacetime? It was practically a trick he had played on them with this death, on the people who had kept him hidden for an entirely different purpose. He didn't need to go into hiding in order to die, he could have just simply . . . , like all the countless others . . .

And then, too, there was a small, all too human disappointment left over: that he had died on them. You don't get the chance to save someone every day. This unacknowledged thought had often helped them carry on when, a little depressed and full of doubt, they thought they couldn't bear this complicated situation any longer and their courage failed them. Always a stranger in your house, someone who never does anything, always someone's fate in your hands, always danger, never free to say and do what you want, never, never, never!

She had secretly imagined what it would be like on liberation day, the three of them arm in arm walking out of their house. Everyone would see right away what he was from his pale face, the color of a shut-in, which his appearance only emphasized even more. How the neighbors and everyone on the street would look when he suddenly walked out of their house and strolled up and down the street with them. It would give them a little sense of satisfaction, and everyone who makes a sacrifice needs a little sense of satisfaction. And then you'd feel that you, you personally, even if only just a little bit, had won the war.

It all had gone up in smoke. It wasn't even a dream anymore. None of the three of them had any luck. But really, him least of all.

Poor Nico!

Hadn't he, on that first night, when Wim said, "Everyone in your situation," answered: "And it's not just Jews . . ."?

It had made them happy to hear those words; he didn't demand any special pity for himself. He stepped modestly back, so to speak, into the circle, the brotherhood of all those who suffer—the same as everyone else, one among many. It was a sympathetic gesture for him to make—a gesture, but not the full truth.

"Actually they're all unlucky."

"Who?"

"The Jews."

They were not in the habit of talking about "the" Jews. If someone was Jewish, that wasn't a problem for them.

"They have it hard," Wim said. "They're like rabbits, hunted. And now it seems like the off-season, when they're safe, is over."

"Why do they let themselves be hunted?"

"What else should they do?" Wim asked. "Run away or let themselves be caught . . . ?"

"And yet they want to keep on being rabbits," Marie said. "Can you understand that?"

"It's their religion," Wim explained.

But Marie protested. She had never been able to tell from Nico that he had anything to do with religion. In truth, even though they were helping to hide one, neither of them understood what it truly meant: a Jew. A human being like everyone else. But . . . But what? It was hard to be so close to someone, to spend so much time in the same house with him, without finally, eventually, asking about his background, about who he was. They didn't want to cause problems and draw boundaries where there hadn't been any before, in their naïve interactions. But both of them would have really liked to know why their Nico was still a Jew. Surely not because other people said so?

"Do you think I could ask him sometime, Wim?"

"If you put it carefully. You never know whether it

might be embarrassing for him. Anyway, even normally, it's kind of a difficult business, asking someone why he's like this and not like that. And kind of a funny question too."

And so Marie, when the occasion arose, while washing dishes in the kitchen, asked him once if he would tell her why he still . . .

"You can tell by looking at me," was his first answer.

Marie shook her head. "In France or in Spain, or even here, in the south near Belgium, no one would notice you."

"Yes, maybe you're right."

"And why didn't you just change countries?"

She'd meant to say "change religions." It was a slip of the tongue. But when she noticed it herself, she didn't correct it.

"First of all, it wouldn't be much help now," he had said calmly, drying a soup plate with big circular motions. "They're taking everyone, even the converts."

Pause.

"And secondly, Nico?" It was almost an interrogation. Except that Marie, the interrogator, was trembling inwardly more than the interrogated.

"And then—ach, Marie, to tell you the truth I've thought about it very, very often. You know, I don't observe any of the customs anymore."

"And why not, Nico. Why didn't you do it?" She imperceptibly turned a little toward him without taking her hands out of the basin.

"And what did he answer then?" Wim asked when Marie told him about the conversation.

"Something very strange. Actually, I don't understand it very well. I almost think it's a little preposterous. He said, 'I always imagined what my father would say about it.'"

"He said that?"

"Yes . . . what his father would say about it."

Wim was silent.

"What do you think of that?"

"I don't think it's as senseless as all that," Wim said after a while.

Marie hesitated.

"To understand it, I would either have to be a son— or have one. Don't you think?" She laughed and stood up a little on her tiptoes.

"Maybe," Wim replied, and he lightly tapped his forehead against hers.

After Marie had finished the usual housework, she came across the laundry bag in the hall on the second floor, clothes still inside as if it had just come from the laundry. With everything else that had been going on in the last few days, she hadn't got around to putting it away. It was a quarter past eleven, and she was thinking that before making lunch she would quickly take out the laundry and put it away in the closet, when Coba appeared.

"Coba?" Marie almost shouted, and all at once she

felt pain again about everything she thought she had put behind her. Her face looked so serious and sad that right away Coba knew everything.

"My God!" —Coba put her hand on her mouth with fright. Five days ago, the last time she was here, he was still alive. So fast! "Tell me," she said, and sat down on the second-to-top step. "Where is he?"

When Marie had finished, Coba fell silent too for a long time. She stared dully into space, and Marie had more than enough time to marvel that someone who was so lively and full of ideas could be so quiet.

"Maybe it's for the best," Coba said at last, and stood up—"best for the two of you and for him . . . poor man." She took off her coat.

"I'll brew up some coffee," Marie said, "but I was just about to put away the laundry. It'll only take a minute. Wim's coming home for lunch."

"I'll help," Coba announced, and slowly climbed the last steps.

She took the laundry out of the bag and gave it to Marie, who put it in the closet.

"What did he have on?" Coba asked, grabbing a tall stack of well-folded shirts of Wim's.

"Pajamas—a pair of Wim's," Marie added, taking the stack of shirts out of Coba's hands and going to the closet.

"I see." Coba bent down again and took hold of a pile of brightly colored terry-cloth towels from the very bottom of the bag. The towels were marked.

". . . I hope you cut off the number from the laundry first." She stood up and waited for Marie, who was still busy at the closet.

"Oh, Coba—" Marie said in a monotone. She felt like she was falling against the closet. She turned around and Coba looked into two wide-open eyes that were filling with fear from one corner to the other, from one second to the next, fear overflowing the eyelids over her whole face and down her neck and running down into her arms and her whole body.

Coba let the towels drop unheeded onto the laundry bag and hurried to the closet. She grabbed Marie's upper arms and stepped right in front of her. All the melancholy memories had vanished, now that there was a new danger.

"Think hard," she whispered, her voice tense; maybe it was a false alarm . . . "Beforehand, did you . . . ?"

Marie closed her eyes and shook her head. In the grip of Coba's two strong, decisive hands, in which she felt all the energy of the other young woman, it was as if every bit of Marie's energy left her. She felt it flowing out of her. "No," she whispered.

"Come here," Coba said, and pulled her onto a chair. "Calm down . . . What a thing to find out!"

When Marie sat down she felt better, but the shock still drained all the strength from her limbs. It came so fast, with no transition, especially after all the weeks and months in which she had had to play the helpful role. Now she felt helpless, utterly ashamed of this new part she so unexpectedly found herself playing, which she had not even started to learn.

On the floor, a little distance away from her, lay the towels, scattered and no longer folded. She could see the laundry numbers in the middle of the top edge, red on white.

"What now?" she asked.

"When does Wim get back?" Coba asked.

"Around noon, quarter past. Do we have that long?"

"I hope so," Coba replied. "I don't know how your police are anyway, are they 'good'?"

"I think so. Wim said something like that."

"Pack up the things you need, I'll tell Wim when he gets home," Coba announced.

Marie let her have her way.

"Hi, Coba, you're here? Where's Marie?" Wim said when he walked into the house a little later. "Did she tell you . . . ?"

"That and something else—" his sister answered. "Listen to this!"

"Dam— . . . is it true?" Wim cried, and turned deathly pale. He began to pace heavily around the room.

"There's no time to lose," Coba said. "I assume your pajamas have not just the laundry number but your monogram embroidered on, as is only proper in any house with a good housewife."

"Of course. I—"

"Never mind. You have to disappear . . . you have to go into hiding."

A short, sharp laugh, like a cough. In the middle of the room he jerked to a complete stop. "Do you have an address for us?" So it had come to this. Now it was their turn. Yesterday still the hosts, giving comfort; today the guests themselves, asking for others' pity . . . !

"There's always a safe house for urgent cases."

"Surely it's . . ." His voice was still bitter. He started wandering around the room again. Suddenly he stopped in front of her. "You're right." He sounded calmer; he had come to his decision. "We have to leave right away. Right away . . . Neither of us thought of the number, it was nighttime, the room was so dark. I didn't either, and I helped her dress him too . . . Well, it doesn't matter. But still, you're careful for a whole year, stay alert like a policeman in your own house, everything goes fine, and then, right at the end . . . It's almost enough to make you laugh!"

"You'll come to my house first," Coba began. "I'll pass you along later."

"Good, Coba, we'll go with you." He had fully regained his old calm and collected attitude.

It was just such a shock! "The whole thing could turn out to be nothing. Our police are almost all good, they're on our side. Who knows?" he concluded. Yes, there was still a chance. Wait and see. "It's just the chief, he's on the other side. Well, we'll see. We'll go with you."

"You can go by bike; Marie and I will take the streetcar."

"Where's Marie?"

"She's upstairs, packing."

When he walked into the bedroom, Marie was just picking up the towels from the floor and putting them away. She was crying.

"I didn't think of it either," Wim said even before she said anything. He wanted to make it clear that it was a problem for both of them together. "Not to mention the doctor. I mean, he doesn't leave his business card in someone's stomach when he operates on him . . ."

Marie had to smile at that last comparison. "What now?" she said timidly. "Did Coba tell you? I've packed everything."

"We'll leave the house right now. I'll bike, you take the streetcar."

"Don't you need to go to the factory?"

"I'll take care of that."

"I'm done."

"Let's go," Wim said.

"I cut out the other laundry numbers, as many as I could—"

Wim interrupted her. "Don't bother. They have a list at the laundry anyway, and some of our other clothes are still there too. Come on, let's go."

While the two women put on their coats in the front hall, Wim walked through the rooms of the house again, to quickly make sure there was nothing else lying around that could compromise them. That was pointless too, in truth, because if the one thing came out it was more than enough to snare them.

When he walked by the little table in the front room, where the vase stood, the thought flashed through his head how quickly, when it's necessary, people can leave behind all the things they possessed in happier times. Exactly as fast as a settled person becomes a refugee. And he heard Nico's voice in his head, telling him how he had left his own apartment.

". . . it was just a two-room sublet, with morning light. I didn't own much furniture that was worth saving. I gave a picture and a few books to a colleague."

"'You can keep them if I don't come back . . .'"

"'I'll keep them safe for you.'"

And Nico went on: "Still, it was painful, like a little twinge. After all, I had lived in that apartment more than ten years. But then I left. I had my suitcase . . ."

Coba stuck her head through the half-open door: "We're leaving. See you at my place." They left.

Wim was alone. The voice kept speaking: ". . . at first I thought, before it happened, that I would not survive it. But then I left. It was fine. As for whether I'll ever be back?" . . . The voice broke off.

Wim understood it better now. He waited a little longer. Then he left. He shut the house door quickly behind him. As for whether they'd ever be back? His bicycle stood there, leaning against the wall of the house, just how he always left it when he came home from the factory. "Like a little twinge, Wim—"

But in any case: It was fine!

XI.

"I can't sit here anymore." Marie sighed, loud enough for Wim to hear her from where he sat next to the other window. She pushed off from the well-worn arms of the chair and heaved herself up. "My back! What am I supposed to do now?"

His legs crossed, right over left and every once in a while changing to left over right, Wim leaned content-edly back in his chair, a bulky volume on his knee: a novel, his second in three days. It took place in Mexico.

"I don't know," he said, as though from another world, and kept reading. Marie waited.

Such an uncanny silence in the building, only rarely the sound of a door opening or closing. Did anyone even live here? It was as quiet as a cemetery.

Had they already buried him? And did they already know . . . ?

They occasionally heard the wailing of sirens. Air raid! Up here on the fourth floor they could hear it especially well. Sometimes twice a day. Now they were coming during the daytime too! A whole orchestra of sirens starting up one after the other. They whipped up excitement; when they were going full strength and ratcheted up higher, your whole body was practically pulled up too, into your ears. And they also awakened sadness and pity, when the air went out of them and the tone fell off and you ran out of breath yourself. Marie was filled with fright. It only reinforced her feeling of being rooted out and hunted.

Then Nico came to her mind again. She *had* understood him. The whole time he was hidden in her house she thought she understood better and better—understood both him and the other thing that stood behind him, invisible, which he embodied—until at last, alone in his room, she got to what was behind his secret too. But now it seemed different to her, as though she herself had entered into this secret in a new way. And she remembered having seen, every once in a while, a flitting in his eyes as though dogs were hounding him.

When she walked up to the closed window and looked steeply down into the little back garden, she was overcome by a kind of vertigo. She leaned her forehead against the glass to feel some support. It started in her eyes, a strange, particular turning and pulling that gradually sucked her whole body into the whirlpool as though she were losing consciousness, while at the same time fear rose within her. "Ridiculous," she said to herself.

But the fear remained, like a tongue of flame suddenly leaping out from some secret fire pit and burning a deep and painful wound in her, so that she almost broke out in tears. She had never felt it like that. She moved quickly away from the window.

"You like it better too, when I don't show my face on the street too much," she started again. Neither of them spent—of course!—the whole day in their room.

But once again came the same answer:

"Yes, better—I mean, it's up to you . . ." He kept reading.

She was plunged still deeper into her indecision. She could see no specific danger in going downstairs either. The truth was, people couldn't tell by looking at them, the way they could tell with Nico, so they didn't have to stay hidden away. It was highly unlikely that the police were already looking for them. Here, in the big city! There were more important things, more significant people, claiming their attention.

But the new role that had so unexpectedly been assigned to her was one that Marie didn't yet know how to play. She felt unsure of herself. To think that he had brought them into a situation like the one he was in when they met him! This uncertainty, increasing from day to day while they waited, while the life they had led up until then slowly crumbled like a mountain eroding away with time until nothing remains but an abyss gaping wider and wider but hidden from sight by the mass of stone deposited there. And even so, their situations were only roughly the same. Cut off from everything they cared about, not knowing if they'd be able to go back, the long waiting, the fear—everything was similar, but their situation only hinted at his. You could hardly compare the two. She didn't regret having made the decision to take him in. But even the best actors can't change from one character into another—unprepared—just like that.

Did Wim feel differently about everything than she did? She would have liked to ask him, but she couldn't put into words the thoughts rushing in on her. And then she also felt that he wasn't being very perceptive, not to say rude. Marie started her wandering through the room. She stepped carefully so as not to be heard in the room downstairs.

The two foldaway beds were put up, hidden behind a large blue curtain that ran the length of the room. The mostly faded wallpaper still showed a few traces of yellow. The mirror with its red wood frame, the chair, the table, and the wardrobe presented every shade from dark brown to light brown. None of the colors matched. Altogether it was like a big spray of wildflowers.

On the opposite wall hung a large picture in an imposing gold frame. A showpiece! A maiden stood in the picture, alone under a tree on a mountain, with a spring storm down below in the valley. Cloud drifts were scattered up the mountainsides, and between them shafts of golden light broke through from some higher place. Maybe they were coming from the gold frame.

Marie stopped in front of it. "How can anyone hang a picture like this of their own free will? Can you understand it, Wim?" She shut her eyes tight, made them into tiny slits, as though raindrops from the storm in the valley were spraying her in the face.

Wim quickly read the line of his book to the end and then held his right index finger on it, like a beginning reader who has to keep the lines from getting all scrambled up.

He couldn't understand it either. "You're right, it's just dreadful." The picture was, in fact, not beautiful. But he really didn't mind it.

"The storm—look, it rained on the painter's palette too."

"It's not a reproduction?"

"No!"

But by then he had pulled back his finger and submerged himself again in the primeval forests of Mexico.

The first day after their hasty departure with Coba, they had landed here, in a family pension run by an older, unmarried woman. The house: an old-fashioned four-story building in a small, dull side street; the residents: older married couples who, scattered throughout the four floors into one or two rooms each, with antiquated furnishings that reeked of never being aired out, mildly endured the frailty of their old age together with furtive, long-suffering patience, and secretly waited, eagerly and full of curiosity, to see which of them would be the first to have to quit the playing field.

"A safe house," Coba had said, and "Such a dear old person."

What sort of dear old friends Coba had! Marie thought, and she kept very skillfully silent during Coba's next visit. In normal times she would have never held out even half a day in this environment.

"She does a lot for us," Coba added with a meaningful look, as though she were already revealing too many secrets, and she left it hanging in the air who this "us" actually was.

"Really?" Wim asked, a little skeptically.

Coba nodded vigorously. Yes indeed!

But it was obviously impossible to reveal any more. And Wim left it at that.

The landlady wore a black dress buttoned up high around her neck, which held her delicate figure as tightly as a soldier's full-dress uniform, and a double-wound gold chain around her neck that hung far down her chest. She walked extremely upright and had an urbane politeness of manner. She was in on the secret. She brought their meals to the room in person.

"My nephew and his wife are coming for a few days," she had told her immediate circle at the beginning: the maid and two of the older couples. Soon the whole pension knew. "They were evacuated. And they are my guests until they have found a new home." And bending closer as though she wanted to whisper, but actually still in a loud voice, because the old people were already a little deaf: "The young woman is in her third month . . ."

Marie and Wim had no idea about any of that; only Coba was in on the plan.

At first Marie was happy just to have a roof over her head. On the second day, she discovered the painting and a few other small color illustrations of dogs' and cats' heads. But the painting seemed to grow bigger and bigger. It hung across from the beds. When they went to sleep at night, it was an evening storm and the virginal maiden had lost her way in the mountains; in the morning, she was already there—she was always the first to wake up—peering down into the valley. On the third day, Marie finally said something. She was losing patience and also beginning to wonder if it had really been necessary to leave their own nice house. Now and then the thought struck her that maybe it might have been possible to find another solution . . .

"Couldn't they also say—" she began again.

"What?" Wim asked, decisively shutting his book. But he still held the tip of his finger pinched between the pages.

Marie was thinking about the milkman, and the baker. And the neighbor woman telling her husband: "Look—next door it's been three days that they haven't been home . . ."

"Oh—"

"Everyone comes and they never answer their door."

"—No, she didn't leave word behind. They must just be head over heels . . ."

"You mean—?"

"Shh, not so loud, the children!"

Marie couldn't stand it anymore. She dashed around the room as though dogs were after her.

Wim followed all her movements with concern. He understood her, he understood her completely. But he couldn't help her. Truth be told, he found it a little childish for her to be so incapable of keeping herself busy. Wasn't she alone all day at home too, when he was at the office? She didn't go out very often then either. He felt sorry for her.

He wanted to try again, more patiently this time.

"Maybe you could sit with me a little?"

"Thank you, but I did just say I can't sit anymore." There were tears in her eyes.

"I forgot," he apologized.

"Forgot," she repeated, contemptuously.

"We have to try to make the best of it," escaped him all of a sudden. He himself was amazed at his words. So clumsy!

"The best of it!" Bitter mockery rang out in her voice.

Patience, Wim said to himself. It was going all wrong. But still, he did find it all a bit boring of her.

"Now, if I had my books here, for example, I'd make such good progress for my exams."

"Oh, you!" He annoyed her with this performance of his alleged laziness.

She sat back down in her armchair.

"But you used to like so much to read," he said gently.

She only looked at him sadly, and bravely gulped back her tears. Pause.

"And you don't have nearly enough socks," she said softly, as though that were the cause of all the unhappiness.

"But I don't need any."

"And I need to wash your shirt."

"I have one more in the closet."

And then suddenly, utterly inconsolably: "I just didn't bring anywhere near enough . . ." But it sounded like: I just had to leave so much behind.

"It's always like that, Marie."

"Yesterday the gas man came by, and today it's the man from the electric company."

"Really? But you know what I really don't like?"

"It's never happened that they've come by and had to wait at the door, with no one to let them in," she went on. She felt a faint fear. What didn't he like about her? It was so unusual, so strange, to sit all day long with a man, with her husband, together in a single room, with him watching her and observing everything. How would other women do? She scrunched up the lace handkerchief in her hand and asked timidly, "What, Wim?"

"That they only show the maiden from the back."

"What maiden is that?"

"There, in the picture!"

He laughed when he saw her baffled face, and the laughter was infectious.

He said, "A back, now that's extremely uninteresting."

But her thoughts had already taken another leap. She couldn't stop thinking about it. "Was it really in the newspaper?"

"I completely forgot to ask Coba."

"Do you think she'll come today?"

"I'm sure she will. She's come every day so far. Maybe—"

"Oh, how long will this last?" Marie sighed.

"How long will this last?" Nico had asked it so many times too, Wim remembered. The same question! In a similar situation! And yet really so different. They still had the possibility that, for example, Coba would appear and tell them that everything was all right.

And all at once Marie shoved her chair closer to his and said, in a wavering voice, "If Nico could see us sitting here . . ."

Wim was startled. He too hadn't been able to help thinking about it. Again and again this thought had pursued him, even deep into the Mexican forests, like a poisonous beast in the thickest underbrush: "If he could see us sitting here!" What would he say? *Marie? Wim? Because of me?* And he turned pale . . . The roles had been switched. The distance between them had narrowed. Now he could take them under his wing. And they understood him better. "I know all about it. It's always like that in the beginning. You get used to it . . ." Wim saw him standing there, almost bodily saw him, with an understanding, slightly sarcastic smile on his tight lips, a wreath of countless wrinkles around the corners of his eyes. But his eyes looked sad. *Because of me?* But when he saw that there was no reprimand in Wim's face, no trace of blame or regret, only the patient readiness of someone who, once he has started something, carries it through to the end, his own features relaxed too. They looked calmly into each other's eyes.

And Marie plucked absently at her handkerchief.

There was a knock at the door and they both jumped up. The elderly woman appeared, in hat and coat, with the four o'clock tea. Marie took the tray out of her hands.

"Aga called," the pension owner said with a friendly smile.

"Aga?" Marie asked. "Who's that?"

"Aga, you know—Coba calls herself Aga on the phone."

"Of course," Wim confirmed. "Understood. And . . . ?" He was burning with curiosity.

"She can't come today, she wanted me to tell you."

"Again, nothing," Marie said, filled with consternation and turning to Wim. "You see."

"Has she been in contact with—I don't know with who, but . . ."

"It's being handled through an intermediary," the dear old woman explained, looking especially nice. It sounded soothing.

"Well then, we'll just have to practice being patient," Wim said, laying his hand gently on Marie's shoulder. She put the tray down on the table in silence.

"Don't worry a bit about your ration cards," the woman explained. "You'll get them no matter what—if it's necessary," she added quickly. "I have to rush off to the train. I'll be back again this evening. Everything's been taken care of."

And walking firmly upright, she left the room.

"I don't believe it," Marie said, falling into a chair. She looked at Wim, completely helpless.

He shrugged his shoulders. Wait it out!

But at the same moment the old woman shut the door behind her, he had the sense that somewhere, invisible in the room, another door was opening, giving him a view out into an unknown distance. While he stood there and looked, a milk-white fog rose up and flooded into the room, overflowing its fixed contours. He had the feeling that everything all around him, even the floor he stood on, was growing vague and in a way contingent. He rubbed his hand thoughtfully over his hair, as though he had to protect it against a suddenly rising wind that was disheveling it. He could feel his heart beating. It had altered its inner rhythm; it beat harder, braver. Then he saw Marie sitting there. She too had receded into the distance and was far away from him, almost unreachable. The way she sat there now, arms pressed tight against her body and hands folded in her lap, alone and full of sadness, she was no longer his wife. There was no connection between them. He saw her as though for the first time. In that moment, this image of her in her foreignness, her otherness, was etched deeply into his mind. He saw she was crying.

"But Marie, you're crying," he said, and he took her hands. The tears ran down her cheeks.

He went on while he tenderly stroked her hands: "What's wrong? . . . Are you scared?"

"I don't know," she whispered back, almost inaudibly.

Silence.

Afterward they drank their tea.

At the same time, the landlady was herself taking steps to make contact. But Coba hadn't told them that. Why should she? The old woman had an even older sister in the town where Marie and Wim lived. For some time, ever since they had started coming and taking men away, this sister had done her part. The task fell to her of making contact with the police officer handling the case of the nighttime find in the park, and finding out all the essential information: whether in fact the police were investigating the clue that had fallen so easily into their hands—the number on the laundry tag.

After she had found out the name of the policeman, and learned at the same time that he was still what was called "a good patriot," she practically stalked him.

It took several days, too long for the two people in the room on the fourth floor.

Gradually Wim stopped taking pleasure in his reading. They went downstairs together and walked around the city, tense and worried. Maybe they would run into someone they knew from their town who would know why they were here. But everything went off without a hitch. No one was looking for them. The weather stayed cold and stormy. Staying in a heated room, near the stove, was still the most pleasant option they had. Soon Wim too grew impatient.

"What do you think, Marie?" he asked one day. "Do you think I can get work from the office to do here?"

Marie shrank back. "But—so you don't still think we'll soon be—"

"No, it's not that," Wim interjected. "That has nothing to do with it. I just meant we have enough work to do at the factory, and I certainly have enough time here."

Marie took it as a sign, though: that he had lost all hope too.

Then, two days later, at an hour when they hadn't expected her, Coba was standing in their room. She laughed with satisfaction.

"Coba!" Marie cried, and rushed toward her. The laugh annoyed her. Was it supposed to mean that now they were really . . . Now that it was here, so suddenly, it was almost impossible to believe.

"What is it?" Wim said in a monotone.

"Everything's all right," Coba answered, stepping closer.

Wim tucked his book under his arm and gripped it so tight that he almost crushed the finger he had stuck between the pages. Still, he waited.

"You can go back."

Marie fell around Coba's neck. Quiet sobbing.

"I know," Coba said, patting her encouragingly on the back. "It took such a long time. And the uncertainty."

"You did it," Wim said, and gripped her hand. He couldn't say anything more. A warm feeling rose inside him; he wanted to be happy and to show that he was happy. But it sounded muted, almost sad.

"It wasn't me," Coba replied, happily excited. "It was the policeman! You were lucky."

So we're going back home, Wim thought to himself. We were lucky. So this warm feeling, with a little grief mixed in, that's luck? They had gained in experience— maybe that's luck?

"I've been so angry with myself," Marie said, still crying, and she let go of Coba's neck.

"But Marie, it was both of us" escaped Wim's lips.

But she shook her head slowly. It was a little celebratory too, since she was also wiping away her tears. No, it was her fault, only hers! The same way she alone knew the secret. Because somehow or other there was a secret connection running between these two events, she just didn't yet know what.

Coba went on: ". . . He cut out the laundry number and the monogram himself and destroyed them as soon as he noticed them. Yes, our police . . . ! He understood right away. Later, when the police chief came, and the coroner, there wasn't a trace."

Wim was silent and bit his upper lip.

But Marie said, after a little pause, "Don't we need to find him and . . ."

"Thank him!!" Coba cried "—Marie! You're . . . ! If you want to, you can send him some flowers after the war!"

After the war! "I'm afraid that'll still be a little while yet," Wim said bitterly. With all the excitement, worries, and day-to-day trivialities, you could almost forget there was still a war going on.

"Now come with me," Coba said decisively. And they packed their little suitcase.

XII.

WHEN THEY CAME HOME LATE ON THE LAST TRAIN, A
little before eleven, the moon's sickle hung in the sky
and cast a dull light. It was bright enough to show that
two people, a man and a woman, were walking there,
but their faces remained unrecognizable.

Marie and Wim liked the half-dark. For they had the
feeling that there was still, even now, something to hide.

Big, dark clouds sailed across the sky, and for a moment, everywhere they looked it was gloomy. A wind
was blowing from the sea. It would bring rain tonight.
But the rain would not find them sleeping.

When they turned the corner, they were hit by the
full strength of the wind coming in from the fields
and across the park. Searchlights in the distance. When
the wind let up, they could hear weak thuds from far
away . . . The airplanes had chosen another route tonight.

The park was empty. Alongside the footpath a chain-link fence, interrupted in only one place. The road led slightly downhill. The last time Wim had walked it . . . Behind the path, as tall as they were and casting deep shadows, were bushes and shrubs, like the darkness itself; farther back, like extinguished candles, were trees and telephone poles. It was like looking at a cemetery.

They found their house just as they had left it. Still, they went inside as though entering something they used to know intimately that had suddenly become unfamiliar. Their happiness too was dampened.

Since they couldn't turn on any lights right away, they felt their way through the dark rooms and hallways to hang the blackout curtains in the windows. Once, they bumped into each other in the dark. They stood for a moment, two warm islands in the cold sea of darkness, facing each other and waiting and calming down. They had had enough adventure. When they started to move carefully through the house again, their arms slightly raised, they reclaimed possession of their things in a new way, different from the way you do when you turn on a bright light the moment you set foot in a house, even before you have walked through a room and straightened a pillow here, tugged at a blanket there.

Afterward, Wim went down to the cellar to get wood for the next day. Marie brewed some coffee. Everything started up again in the ordinary way they were used to. They felt abashed and a little lonely; even though they didn't say anything about it, each noticed it in the other.

Then Wim wound the clock back up and reset it to the right time. And with every half hour and hour that chimed while Wim was gently pushing the hand around with his finger, they too returned as though to a new day.

It was almost midnight.

"Tomorrow morning early, as usual?" Marie asked.

"Seven-thirty. Come up to bed!"

As they climbed the steps to their bedroom and walked past "his" door, they shyly and silently looked at the brightly painted wood. The black door handle remained at the horizontal, as always.

But it seemed to them both that the door was closed in a way it had never been closed before.